Lies &

Deceit

A Novel By

Angela Murray

GRAND ROYALE PUBLISHING

ISBN-13: 978-0-9960150-0-4
ISBN-10: 0996015000

Library of Congress Control Number
    2014936551

For information on bulk purchases, please visit:
www.grandroyalepublishing.weebly.com
Or contact Email: grpbooks@yahoo.com
Grand Royale Publishing
P.O. Box 86
Docena, Al 35060
Typeset by Rukyyah and cover designed by for Erotic Ink Designs
Edited by Rukyyah

Printed in United States of America
10 9 8 7 6 5 4 3 2 1

DEDICATION

MISSED TREMENDOUSLY—MEMORIES FOREVER

This book is dedicated to my grandmother Mary Rucker, the wind beneath my wings, my strength and my rock.

To my grandmother Fannie Wagner and my Aunt Lillie Mae, two women that taught me how to be compassionate and have unconditional love towards people. Missing you both.

My nephew Kennis Rucker, he 'always' allowed me to tell him my dreams and made me feel special all the time. I will love and will miss you forever.

This is for my Aunt Lola that believed in me from day one and told me to just do it. I've met many people but none with the grace and character you portrayed even when the chips were down.

My Uncle Willie, my second father that loved me in-spite of my head strong ways. He always taught me to work hard and respect myself. He always told jokes that would make you think—His favorite saying 'I will give it to you the second Saturday of next week". LOL.

My sister/friend through God, Roneshia 'Trenea' McCray, you were an inspiration to all and you will hold a place in many hearts for years to come. Miss you.

ACKNOWLEDGEMENTS

First, all credit and praise must go to the highest God Almighty. Without him none of this would be possible. Through all my trials and tribulations he has been there when nobody else would. I give him much thanks and many praises.

To my mother, Rosia and my father Nathaniel thanks for all the love and great genes that has made this possible for me. Love the both of you and I wouldn't trade you for nothing here on earth.

To my three joys in life, my kids: Brian, Christopher and Brianna. Thanks for sticking with me on this journey. Times may have been tough but we finally made it. To my wonderful granddaughter Ivyanna, grandmother loves you to pieces. And my words to each of you, "Remember YOU can DO and be ANYTHING you set your mind on as long as you have the desire, determination and dedication."

To my sisters and brothers, Yolanda, Felicia, Bernadette, Nathaniel and Roderick, thanks for allowing me to talk and express myself all the time. The love I have for each of you is immeasurable.

To my aunts and uncles, Shirley, James, Arthur Lee, Carolyn, L.C., Susan, Ann and Big Boi thanks so much for all the support and advice. I love each of you so very much.

To my sweet nieces and nephews, Tee Tee Ann-gee love you all, Brittany, Kennis (RIP), Brinia, and Natasha, Cyla, Amya, Khalia, Charity, Christian and Jamya, Christian, Adarius, Kennard(and his two lovely daughters). To all my younger cousins Tee Tee Anngee loves you all.

To all my cousins, Cynthia, Cee-Cee, Cedric, Trice, T.J., Earl, Bernard, Jackie, Moochie, Bo-Bo, Anna, Alex even though we're cousins we all act like sisters and brothers. I love you all. To all my other cousins I love you all just as much.

If I didn't mention your name, trust me I didn't leave it off intentionally. I want you all to know that your love and support is greatly appreciated also.

Thanks Erotic Ink Publishing (Rukyyah) for such a great book cover and the first editing. Thanks for ALL your patience and understanding. It was such a joy to work with you on my first book.

Most of all I would like to thank all of my readers, book buyers for without you this could not be possible. I love you all and hope when I'm in your city; you come out and support a sister. Tell your family, friends and coworkers to get the book.

ALWAYS FOLLOW YOUR DREAM BECAUSE YOUR POT OF GOLD IS AT THE END OF THE RAINBOW ALSO........*

Chapter One

If Loving You Is Wrong I Don't Want To Be Right

As twenty year old Mercedes Alee'ya Watson pulled her 2013 black on black fully loaded Range Rover SUV into one of her parent's four car garages and turned the ignition off. All she could do was throw her hands in the air, and say, "I own the world." Something, she heard often in the past six years. Being that her father was Pastor Franklin Watson of Greater Miracle Church of God, one of the largest and fastest growing churches' in the city of Atlanta. He already had thirty-five hundred members and memberships were steadily growing. He was about to branch out into television ministry, which would easily add a few extra thousand members while adding much more cash to the already overflowing tithing and offering baskets. Mercedes felt the more members, the bigger her daddy's bank account would be and the more she would have to spend on splurging. Splurging was something she loved and something she did often on Pastor's black credit card.

'I Own the World' was a phrase that Pastor Watson preached often behind the closed doors of his six and a half million dollar, twelve thousand-five hundred, square foot lavish home that sat on over three acres of land. His home was located on the outskirts of Atlanta in a very upscale gated community. It was a community of who's who on the A-list of people that made well over six and seven figure salaries a year, an upscale, elite community that made you feel as though you'd reached the status of 'I've made it'. A lifestyle that made outside people think you were a celebrity and anxious to snap photos as you drove past. This was a home Pastor Watson and First Lady Tiffany Watson had designed with the most lavish, exquisite top of the line materials, and furniture. First lady loved the finer things in life and every opportunity she got she purchased something lavish and expensive. Pastor and First Lady always drove the most expensive cars, ate at five stars, white linen restaurants, shopped at upscale designer stores, and traveled to cities you see in magazines. One would say they lived the life of the rich and famous and they lived up to the meaning of just that, rich and famous.

The Pastor and First Lady walk-in closet housed nothing but top designer clothes, shoes, jewelry, purses, and furs. Just entering you felt as thou you were strolling down Rodeo Drive in Beverly Hills. Everything was organized by color, style, and season. Nothing was worn twice in a year and there were plenty of items that still had price tags hanging from them. One thing Pastor and First Lady agreed upon was that they would make sure they purchased items they knew their members would never be able to afford. First Lady cringed at the thought of walking out in the congregation to greet a member wearing or having anything she owned. She wanted to be the only one giving the latest most expensive fashion from head to toe. It was something she strived for each and every day, but Sunday's were her show off days. Sunday mornings was the day she

Lies & Deceit

spent extra time making sure she dressed like she was ready for a photo shoot for the Ebony magazine cover. She would always make an entrance in church that made the other females in the room want to be like her, but yet and still wanted to hate her guts. But, most came to love her because of her soft feminine ways. Always kind, nice, soft spoken and giving. Well giving of advice never money. She felt handouts only made you lazy, so any monetary gifts given were earned. She lived by the Chinese Proverb that said, 'Give a man a fish, he eats for a day. Teach a man to fish, and he eats for a lifetime.

Mercedes Alee'ya Watson age twenty, she was Pastor Watson's oldest of two daughters. She loved lavish expensive items just like her mother, but for the life of her she didn't want to live up to her father's standards of doing the right thing. She tried her best to pretend to be the Christian young lady he thought he'd raised. But, she cringed at the thought that her father wanted her and her seventeen year old sister A'Lexus A'miya Watson to be the perfect preacher's daughters. Well, she intended to do just as the people on the street said about preacher's daughters. Get buck wild and enjoy all the things he preached against. Only because she felt he tried to force the word on them. Something they both rebelled against.

Mercedes was cute, smart, and crafty all at the same time. She was five feet eleven inches without heels. She had warm caramel, flawless skin complexion, long silky jet black hair that had the texture of Indian hair that fell right past her shoulders, and smoky hazel brown eyes. She had a very well-proportioned figure that caught many men's attention because of her perfect 36C cup breast, a slim waist that accentuated her round 38 hips. She often wondered if she was Pastor biological daughter because there was no resemblance of Pastor or First Lady. Pastor stood about five feet six inches with a very chocolate complexion and hair like wool, which he kept closely cut to his scalp. Looking at Pastor one would say he might have had a fast hard life that somewhere came to a crossroad and he did a detour to God because he only had two choices jail or hell. First Lady was about five feet four inches tall with a very warm chocolate flawless even tone skin complexion with deep black eyes and the same curvy figure she had when she was in her early twenties. Mercedes was always told she looked like her great aunt on her mother's father side of the family. But being that First Lady didn't grow up knowing her father or his family she never was able to produce a picture. So Mercedes took their word as being truth.

She was a junior at Spelman College located outside of Downtown Atlanta, majoring in Psychology. She chose psychology because she wanted to learn why Pastor acted the way he did, but better yet to learn how to deal with his sometime demonic ways. Sometime, she thought about studying to become a psychiatrist because she felt Pastor and First Lady most definitely were crazy at times. And she wanted to understand her father and mother's imbalance.

College was Mercedes home away from home to open up and do the things her father preached against. She could party, drink, smoke, stay out all night and date whomever she wished to date as long as she covered her tracks and attended Sunday services. She knew there was a thin line between loving her secret sneaky ways and hating her conniving lies she told her parents. But, she realized that lying was the only way she could continue her escapade. She was home for summer break and knew she had to step up her game of lying in order to do the things she did in college with no parental restrictions. She loved summer break, but hated the fact that she had to go back home with her parents for those three long months, which normally got her in plenty of trouble because of the many rules and restrictions that her parents enforced. But, she always managed to get through the summer and back to her campus mischievous lifestyle a little bit earlier, by making up lies that there was early registration and they always fell for it.

Mercedes and A'Lexus were spoiled beyond spoiled. They wanted for nothing and as long as they followed Pastor Rules, their wish was his command. The Bibles verse, 'you spare the rod, you spoil the child,' had its own meaning in the Watson's house. From the looks of things Pastor was preaching one thing and practicing something totally different. Because the girls were most definitely spoiled rotten and had never endured a spanking. The only form of punishment was a stern loud voice as they reached puberty and their hormones were raging out of control. Pastor was always the strict disciplinarian in the home. First Lady was always silent, looking away as if they weren't her own flesh and blood. As the girls got older she would succumb to the master bedroom and rarely came out to console or just check on them. Mercedes and A'Lexus bond grew stronger because of First Lady's lack of maternal instinct and knew they had to stick together, especially the way Pastor would carry-on sometimes with his loud fussing and cursing.

As Mercedes got out the SUV, she remembered she had been to Victoria Secrets and Erotic Lingerie in the Downtown Buckhead area to purchase a few novelties for later with her man. She knew she couldn't bring those bags in at that time or they would really cause havoc in the holy sanctified Pastor Watson's house. Per Pastor Watson, that was considered a whore's wardrobe. Only strippers, prostitutes, and jezebels indulged in such attire. And anyone indulging in that behavior was surely to go to hell quick, fast, and in a hurry. He would describe hell as being the worst place anyone would want to live. But, she often felt like the Watson's home was hell on wheels in high gear with all the rules, arguing, and punishments.

As she went to the trunk of the SUV she decided to take the items she had bought and place them in the oversized Louis Vuttion overnight bag she carried as a purse until she got to her bedroom. A room located on the west wing of the house, the size of two master bedrooms that had gorgeous crown molding, a chandelier shipped in from France, a fireplace with Italian marble surrounding its mantle, three arched windows that faced the landscape garden out on the back of the home that showed off the lavish pool. The room she knew was off limits to her parents. A room she had Pastor to pay over five thousand dollars to decorate. The colors were pink and green the colors of the AKA sorority. A group she so desperately wanted to pledge before she got to college, but her late nights and extra-curricular actives kept her to busy for any type of sorority commitment. But, what she told Pastor and

First Lady you would have thought she was the president of the organization. One lie led to another and from her story she had crossed over and was very active in the organization. She felt what they didn't know wouldn't hurt them. So she lied every time they questioned her about the sorority.

Mercedes also hid the fact that she was dating Roc. He was one of the biggest dope dealers in the city and everybody gave him the respect as if he was the mayor of the city. It most definitely wasn't Roc's money that kept her nose wide open, but the mere fact that she pulled something over on her father that kept her adrenaline pumping for more of her man's love and time. Roc wined, dined, and treated her like she was a princess in the beginning, but he did have a mean streak about him and could tell some convincing lies, that later came out about three months into the relationship. Even though Pastor wined and dined her like she was a princess, too, Roc's attention was totally different and she loved him in spite of his temper, late nights and drug dealing. Being in college and living on campus was the advantage that she had to do the sneaky things she did under Pastor's nose. Once on campus she partied and did all her naughty activities because there she was considered a grown ass woman with no curfew, no rules, and no responsibilities.

It was summer break and she had to return home, which meant a lot of her extra-curricular activities would be on pause until she came up with a plan that wouldn't bring any attention to her wrong doing. Skimming was something that came easy to her. She didn't know if it was because her father was so strict and she had to find ways to out trick him, or because it was a gene she had inherited from one of her parents. A past lifestyle they weren't sharing. Either way, Mercedes knew she couldn't live under Pastor's roof for the entire three months and follow all of his rules. She could follow some, but not the entire list that he had posted on a plaque for all to see in the main hall. Rule number one was an easy rule. 'You must pray at all time in the Watson's home.' She prayed alright, praying that he would change his ways. But, she knew as long as she covered her tracks and stayed out of his path, she would be able to live in a little peace.

As Mercedes entered into the massive gourmet kitchen she saw in her dad's eyes the eagerness to see what she had bought with all his money. As she walked over to the oversized kitchen granite top island and laid the bags down it wasn't a hot second before Pastor started rambling through her bags. But, she made sure she kept her oversized Louis Vuttion bag on her shoulder because she knew if he seen the vibrators, scented body lotion, edible panties, whips, chains, and diamond studded handcuffs, the devil was surely to be unleashed by her preaching pastor father. Plus, those things were only to be seen and used by her and her man Roc.

"Mercedes, baby, you been out all day long and this is all that you got a pair of pantyhose, two very expensive dresses, and four pair of shoes for church? What have you been doing all day long? And, from the looks of it you didn't bring your old man anything. I thought you loved me baby girl," Pastor said, trying to pretend he was upset. But, later gave a smirk of a smile like he was just joking.

"Daddy, please don't start with the whining because you know I love you and wouldn't take nothing for you –well except a million dollars," Mercedes said, laughing and her mother chimed in with a soft giggle.

"Baby, you would take a million dollars for me."

"Naw daddy they would have to give me about ten million dollars because I love you that much not to except no million," she said, laughing while grabbing up her bags. She walked out the kitchen towards her bedroom. All the while trying to hurry from the kitchen before Pastor started prying into her school life. Something she wasn't up to talking about since she hadn't been to class the last few weeks before school ended for the summer. Well maybe off and on for those last few weeks.

Ring, Ring,

Her cell rang over and over in her purse. As she pulled it out, she looked down at the caller ID and realized that the number was her man. She smiled from ear to ear because she knew exactly what he wanted. Her, totally butt naked. All she could do was smile, thinking about what the night entailed. Love making 101, 102, 103, and then a refresher course.

"Hey, baby. Where are you?" she said softly into the phone. Trying not to talk loud and be heard.

"Laying up in this king size bed, dick hard as a rock waiting on my baby to come and fuck my brains out," Roc said with a husky tone.

She felt rather nervous because each time she talked to him on the phone in her parent's house she felt his voice carried over rather loud and they could hear every word he said. And, those were not words that should be said in a preacher's house, especially from a thug to a preacher's daughter. But, she anticipated each phone call from him because they consisted of phone sex. How he wanted to fuck her, where he wanted to fuck, and when he wanted to fuck her. They had probably used about three hundred positions in their eight month relationship. She lost count after number twenty. With her being twenty, all she thought about was fucking. She studied more on how to please her man than passing her exams for class.

Mercedes was rather hesitant about dating Roc, but there was thug love running all through her veins. Each time she tried to love a church boy she couldn't relate because they were to easy going, always wanting to please and pretending to be a Christian, preacher-boy type, always saying he saving himself for the right woman. With that being said, she knew she wasn't the right woman to put up with that bull. She needed someone to challenge her mentally and sexually. She loved a challenge. A challenge that sent you on goose chases, dark dirt roads, other bitches' houses, parking lots, in the cut waiting to start trouble. That kind of thug, gangsta-lying love, that broke your heart every chance it got. That gangsta shit that you knew would eventually get you in trouble. Roc was that type of gangsta guy that lie to you and you know it's a lie but you still believe him. But the way he said it and the emotions he put with it made you question his story in the back of your mind, but never verbally calling him out on his lie. Just believing his every word even if the truth was right there slapping you in your face. Just loving and living in denial because he was your man. In a relationship where you trust his every word until he finally gets tired of you. Always that ride or die chick, he can't do any wrong in your eyesight, because you forgive, and try to forget. You forget only long enough until something else happens. But in the end we forgive and love them once again.

The night she was at Greenbrier Mall on the east side of town. An area her father had summoned her and her sister to never frequent she met Roc. He pulled up in the Quick Stop-gas station as she was about to pump her gas. Rambling through her purse feverously looking for her credit card, as she always did because she never put anything back where she found it, but the sound of his car distracted her and caught her attention. He revved the engine as if he was trying to bring attention to himself. Startled, Mercedes leaned up and caught a glimpse of a handsome somewhat thuggish guy. As he got out the car, she noticed he was about six feet six inches tall, medium body-build yet masculine, low cut, and neatly trimmed hair. He was dressed in the latest Akoo designer jeans with a matching Akoo tee shirt, Lebron sneakers, and a Falcons' cap. He was very coordinated and she could smell the scent of Usher's cologne he wore. The cologne was a smell she loved on any man. As she went back to rambling in her purse, she felt a tap on her shoulder that startled her and from the way it was done she thought, oh my God! I'm getting robbed. Damn it! Pastor warned me about being over in this area. But, her nostrils were filled with the scent of the Usher cologne and she quickly turned to notice it was him. She tried hard not to look eager, but before she could say anything, he pushed three hundred dollars in her hand.

"Take this and fill up. If anything is left, get you something to drink," he said in a husky deep tone.

She gently pushed the money back at him and had a look that said she had money. "Thanks but no thanks I can buy my own gas." She said as she slyly got a glimpse of him before he turned and started to walk back towards his car.

He turned and looked at her. "I never said you couldn't and the way you looking in that purse you just might get robbed out here so take the money, pay for your gas, and get out of this neighborhood because you don't belong over here."

She gave a slight right eye squint and put a serious look on her face as she turned to him, thinking, how dare him to say I don't belong over here. What make him think this about me? She thought something was wrong with her since everybody was talking like Pastor, giving her orders when she was fully grown. Telling her things like: Don't go here. Don't do this. Put this back. Sit over here. Just rule after rule.

"You don't know where I belong and what is it to you anyway. I'm grown and can go and do as I please," she blurted over at him with much attitude.

"Yeah you grown alright, but can you handle being grown?" He jokingly said as he started his engine and revved it once again.

"Like I just said, I'm grown and can do as I please." She smart mouthed, but in a jokingly way this time.

"Well Ms Grown, put my number in your cell and call me later. 555-1436," he yelled over the loud music playing on his system. She could hear every word sung by B.O.B. blasting out his loud speakers and she had to catch herself because she swayed to the music, but she caught his number even with the loud music blasting. He put the car in drive, turned around to look in her direction, and yelled back, "you know you mine now, so don't ever forget that shit girl."

Her first thought was, how the hell can he say that he own me by giving me three hundred funky dollars? She knew right then he didn't know who she really was—she was the heiress to the Watson's Millions. She didn't really need his money, but deep down she knew she really wanted to try his love. He was the type of man she was waiting to hook up with and she knew that she could get down with his thuggish ways. As he peeled out the parking lot leaving smoke from the burning rubber of the tires, she smiled and put his number in her cell. Never in her wildest thinking would she have guessed he was too much for her just like that fast Lambo he was pushing. That night was the first of many good and bad nights to come for her new found relationship.

Speaking into the receiver Mercedes smiled ear to ear. "Baby, I have to spend a little time with my family and as soon as I can break away all this is yours. All yours baby," she said with a smile so big, showing off her pearly white perfect teeth. She felt dental hygiene was very important. She couldn't stand seeing a want to be chick with a raggedy mouth. This was a total turnoff to men, well the one's that looked for a trophy girl not the booty call chicks, the one night stands or the backseat blow job ratchet chicks. The one he wants to introduce to his mother, make his wife and be the mother to his kids had to be on top of her appearance game and profession.

"Shit, how much longer I have to wait? I'm about to explode. Damn, girl I need you right fucking now. You can't tell them you need to run to the store and come give me a quickie? You got me all hard and shit, plus you talking about you need to spend time with your parents. What about me and my needs?" Roc replied as he reached down between his legs and gently massaged his engorged penis.

"What I have for you can't be done in 'NO' quickie. I promise to make it up to you when I get there. I have some toys that will make you cum all over the place. Just give me a few more minutes, I promise I will make it all up to you. I love you boo." She said as she rubbed between her legs while thinking about all her little novelties she had splurged on at the mall.

"O.K., baby. Do what you gotta do. Me and ole boy will be here when you get done. Just hurry up because I need you bad," he said as he reached over to grab the pillow and placed between his legs.

As Mercedes hung up the cell, A'Lexus entered the room, looking rather stressed. A look she had more often since she started smelling herself. Something the older people would say about teenagers who wanted to be grown before their time.

"What up girl? Look like somebody's has pissed you off," Mercedes said as she rolled over on the bed and tossed the pillow in A'Lexus direction.

"Daddy is getting on my fucking nerves! I'm so tired of his bullshit. He's always preaching shit that gets on my last nerve. I will be so damn glad when I get grown so I can leave this damn house" A'Lexus said as she joined Mercedes on the bed, laying on her back as she looked up at the ceiling, looking totally stressed out.

"Girl, you know you can't be cursing up in this holy house. Don't you know God is watching your every move and what you do in the dark will eventually come to the light? You will be punished in the pit of fire in hell if you continue," Mercedes said, laughing loudly and sounding just like her preacher father.

"Sometime I think you taking the wrong major in college because you sound just like the Pastor all sanctified and shit," A'Lexus said, sounding a little relieved that she had her big sister to talk to at times of frustration. But, a lot of times that didn't solve the problems lurking in the Watson's home.

"A'Lexus, I need a favor and before you hold your hand out for some money let me tell you what first. I don't need you getting pissed with me and ratting me out to Pastor." Mercedes said as she sat up and looked A'Lexus right in her big brown eyes.

"If the price isn't right you can forget it. Daddy has taken my allowance because he said I didn't show up for the youth revival. He hasn't realized that I'm not his sweet little innocent baby girl anymore. I'm fucking 17 years old, almost graduated and damn grown. What I look like at youth revival with all those lil' ass kids?" She blurted out as she fell back on the bed, grabbed a pillow, and pretended to be suffocating herself.

Mercedes reached over and grabbed the pillow from her face, tossing it in the corner. "You look like his lil' spoiled bratty baby girl," Mercedes said, laughing as she got up off the bed and headed toward the walk-in closet. The closet was huge and every space was filled with expensive designer clothes, purses, shoes, scarves, and jewelry. There were clothes that still had the price tag from the prior year.

Mercedes bought things because she could and not because she needed any of the items she purchased. Most were rarely worn twice and many were purchased just to flaunt because a majority of her college friends couldn't afford to shop at the high end stores and boutiques she frequented. Most of the girls looked up to her because she rocked the latest most fashionable designer items. It was all about status with her when it came to pissing off some of the girls that hated her guts, especially the sorority girls. Even the doctor's daughters or multimillion dollar business owner's kids couldn't keep up with her fashion. She felt you had to have grown up knowing fashion and wearing it every day to be a fashionista. Not coming into money in the middle of the game and trying to live that life. First Lady made sure the girls were in the most expensive top name clothes coming up so it made it easy for them to know and appreciate the finer things in life. First Lady taught them you dress to impress, and taught them that if they wanted to be in the most elite groups, the first impression should be glamorous and flawless. And, your attitude and personality should match the look. She also told them that flattery would get them far, but their looks would be the key to getting them through life.

"O.k. Heifer, you need me so I suggest that you be on my side and stop badgering me about being spoiled. Because you know I learned from the best." She said as she got off the bed looking over in Mercedes direction as she walked toward the window.

"Ok, spoiled brat". Mercedes said jokingly as she pushed A'Lexus on the shoulder in a playful manner. "I need you to drop me off at Roc's house tonight. And I need you to come back home fall asleep forgetting to come pick me up. In the morning tell daddy that you overslept and forgot to come and pick me up. But I'm going to tell them that I'm going over to A'saabi apartment to help with the young educator's seminar and you want to borrow the Range Rover."

"So you still mess around with that thug. He ain't worth the time of day Mercedes. All he wants you for is one thing. Sex."

"And?"

"And, you better than that. You got too much going for you to throw it all away for sex, drugs, crime, and baby momma's. Don't you want more out of life than to be dealing with his low life activities? He means you no good and I literally mean NO GOOD!" she belted out at her sister. She cringed every time Mercedes mentioned his name or talked about how much she loved him. She had heard around town, he was the low life of all thugs. He cared about nothing, but himself and always treating people wrong. He had acquired a name for himself in Atlanta and it wasn't a very pleasant one.

"See A'Lexus that is what you don't know. He loves me and only me. Girl with all the sex that I be putting on him, he don't have time to fuck NOBODY else. I'm his everything. He's lying in bed butt naked with a long hard on waiting on Moi –me in French, if you didn't know," Mercedes said with a big grin on her face. Posing in the mirror, admiring herself because she knew she was beautiful.

"So are you going to do it?" Looking over at her sister with a sad puppy dog look knowing she couldn't say no as she waited on her response. The look that made A'Lexus give into anything her sister wanted done.

Rolling her neck and snapping back with an attitude as usual, especially when she was pissed with her father. "So what's in it for me?"

"Girl, you know I got your back on anything. Whatever you need I got you. Promise." As she leaned in to give her little sister a hug, A'Lexus quickly turned away in a playful manner as the two of them laughed.

Giving Mercedes the attitude side eye to the left letting her know it came with a big price "O.k. and don't forget that shit when I need you. Just remember you owe me big time."

Mercedes went into the large oversized bathroom to take a shower and to get dressed for her night with her man. A'Lexus resorted back to her bedroom to figure out a few things on how she would handle Pastor and the lying scheme Mercedes had concocted.

An hour later, Mercedes had transformed into a sweet little church going daughter, who had innocence written all over her. But, she knew she was a wolf dressed in sheep clothing. Once she shredded the first layer of clothing she would be transformed back into the devilish college student with all the bad habits.

As Mercedes and A'Lexus were about to leave, Pastor Watson came storming into the bedroom door preaching as usual. This was an every time event, even after he had approved for them to go out he had to stir things up. "Mercedes, you may go to college and live on campus, but that don't make you grown. What you do wrong will eventually catch up with you young lady. And, Miss A'Lexus don't think for one minute because you have a big sister you can do and go like her. You ain't grown and won't be for a long time. So you drop her off, go straight to the library, and get back home 'til it is time to pick your sister up. Do you both understand me?" His nostrils were spread wide and he had this evil vein running down the middle of his forehead as he spoke in a very authoritative voice. He used his stern loud voice as if it was to put fear in them. But A 'Lexus and Mercedes had become use to it and they always pretended to be in fear to throw him off. And it worked every time.

Mercedes just shook her head because for the life of her she could not figure out why her father was so crappy. Always talking about how God had taken him from near death and blessed him with the finer things in life. How he had been changed and given another chance at life and a good life. How he was placed here to rule the world. She thought he had gotten that concept mistaken. Not the world he should be ruling but her and her baby sister.

Pastor turned to walk out, but as usual he had to have the last word. "Tomorrow is Sunday and I expect the both of you at church bright and early. And if either one of you come stumping in church late, I promise you that you will regret it." He walked out the door and walked down the hall towards his office.

A'Lexus' blood had begun to boil and she rolled her eyes so hard you would have thought she was having a spastic attack. "Mercedes girl! That old man is getting on my last nerve! He is always bickering about something. He ain't nothing but a Pimp in the Pulpit. Pimping folk out their money with all those rehearsed sermons. You just don't know how bad I want to get out of this house."

"A'Lexus, girl. You will be out sooner than you think. You only have another year and a couple of months before you will be on a college campus far away from this saga. Believe me it will be here sooner than you think just give it time," Mercedes said, trying to calm her sister and give her some logical sister to sister advice.

As they got into the vehicle and started up Mercedes popped in TI's new CD and blasted the song Can You Love a Troubled Man? Featuring R. Kelly. She loved that song because it spoke volumes about her and Roc's relationship. She belted out the words so loud; you could barely here the CD. Every time it got to the end she hit replay. After the fourth time listening to it, A'Lexus forwarded to the song Hello featuring Cee-lo Green, one of her favorites. They rode the entire ride with the windows down blasting the CD and singing along.

As they approached their destination Mercedes reached in the back of the SUV and grabbed her overnight bag she had placed in the car earlier. She had done this so Pastor wouldn't suspect any fowl play in their plan. She needed to spruce up her makeup, and do a quick wardrobes change. She left the house with a going to church outfit but she had a jaw dropper, tongue wagging, eye bulging, sexy cat suit she purchased to make her man appreciate what the lord gave her. She had been blessed with a fine body with some good goodies. As she finished with the last touches of her hair and makeup she looked over to A'Lexus to get the sister approval that she looked damn good.

"OK, A'Lexus, don't forget that you forgot to pick me up. I've already schooled A'saabi on the situation. And if daddy wants to call me, it's not a problem. My phone will ring over to A'saabi's cell and she will answer like it's my phone and tell him I'm either in the bathroom or ran to the corner store and I will call him back. Love you and be careful," Mercedes said as she hugged and kissed A'Lexus on the cheek before exiting the vehicle.

As Mercedes walked up to the door her thought was 'damn I feel for only children. They don't have anybody to help them with lies. I love my sister and I wouldn't take a million dollars for her not even ten. And I know she love me the same.'

Chapter Two

Can't Nobody Love Me Like He Can

"Baby, is that you?" Roc yelled from upstairs. "Baby, is that you?" he yelled again as he reached over by the nightstand drawer where he kept his piece. If it came to blasting a nigga, he had no problem with doing just that.

"Honey, it's just the preacher's daughter," Mercedes said as she entered the room, doing her seductive dance to the stripper song.

"Damn, girl! You were just about to get some lead in yo' ass and I ain't talking about this pipe I'm packing," Roc said as he reached down, grabbed his dick, and moved in closer to his baby. Mercedes was dancing and moving seductively and she knew it was working because she could see the bulge rising in Roc's pajamas. She knew if her father knew just how devilish she was, she would be shipped off to a missionary program in Africa faster than an overnight UPS delivery.

"Girl, you make a brother wanna go to church and pray that this shit never end. How in the hell did a preacher daughter learn to fuck and suck a nigga's shit so damn good?"

"I learned by reading sex books and watching x-rated movies, and performing them on you." Mercedes said, grinning as she leaned down and kissed his lips.

"They say the best women are in the church. Just freaks. But, I ain't complaining," he said as he guided her hands to his hot throbbing rod.

"I'm going to be your freak all night long. Your wish is my command," she said as she reached in her bag and took out her lil' toys. Some she purchased at the novelty store and many she purchased from the Kandi Bedroom's collection. She could see the big grin planted on Roc's face, looking like it was his first time. That was one thing he really loved about Mercedes because she always brought excitement and a variety to the bedroom. She always came to please to the ultimate sexual level.

She got up and placed the scented candles strategically around the room and lit them. She turned on some soft, love making music. She then took the mask and placed it over his eyes, took his arms, and pulled them over his head. She put the diamond studded handcuffs on; took out her scented lotion, and gently rubbed all over his body as she gently kissed him in all his sensuous spots. And she knew it aroused him because each time she kissed a spot, his erected dick would jump and one or two times she would have her mouth right there to tease with it. Roc was so caught up in what she did, he never realized that her friend Porsha had entered the room and had joined in on the lovemaking. Neither Mercedes nor Porsha intended to fill him in on what was about to happen. As a matter of fact, it was not the first time they had done some shit like that to Roc or any other brother they were sex'n. Porsha never really had actual sex with him, but she did everything else that would lead him up to wanting to stick his dick in her pussy. Mercedes would be sucking on his long throbbing dick while Porsha was in a 69 position letting him eat, lick, and suck on her pussy. They would even swap position and he never suspected a thing being that they both basically had the same body build.

"Damn girl you can change the pull on your fucking jaws. How you do that shit?" he said in between the changes of Porsha and Mercedes. But, she would say some simple shit like, 'I've learned what my dick like, so I give it what it want and need baby.' Anything to keep him satisfied."

After about thirty minutes of hot foreplay, Porsha exited the room without Roc even knowing she had been there with them and to let Roc do what he do best. Fuck the shit out of Mercedes in every possible position.

Mercedes moaned softly as Roc slowly made love to her body. She arched her back and held his hips as she rode each gyrating grind. Their lovemaking had gotten to a point that it was so hot, steamy and passionate that Mercedes prolonged climaxing. Roc was slow grinding and each time she got to the point of reaching a climax, he would pull out, giving her enough time to calm down for the next round. After about thirty minutes of him tantalizing and teasing her body, he reached over and grabbed Mercedes pulling her on top of him allowing her to show off her skills. Mercedes rode him in a way that made his body tense up and arch up close to her as he exploded inside her, but caused him to scream like a bitch getting beat by her pimp when his body ejaculated. As she was rolling off the top of him, Roc grabbed her, pulling her close to his body and held her like she was a baby.

"Girl I wouldn't take a paying job for you. I love you baby and I'm going to hustle these damn streets to keep you happy because ain't no 9-5 going to keep my baby happy with the finer things of life," Roc said as they lay in each other arms. The only thing he knew was that she had the best pussy and fucking techniques he had ever come across. He may not love her the way she wanted to be loved, but he knew she was a keeper for the moment. She was the perfect fit for his plans to move his drugs and build his empire.

As Mercedes lay in Roc's arms, never once did she think about the consequences of getting caught. All she knew was she was happy and nobody or nothing could change that feeling. But, before falling off to sleep, she said a little prayer. Even though she did her dirty scandalous sneaky acts she always prayed.

****

It was 9 a.m. Sunday morning and A'Lexus still hadn't come to pick up Mercedes. She had called A'Lexus cell phone several times, but there was no answer. She had called A'saabi phone and there was no answer. She started to worry that something had happened to her dad or her mom. It even crossed her mind that A'Lexus and her dad had gotten into another heated argument and A'Lexus had done the unthinkable. She had killed Pastor Watson.

Mercedes was caught between a rock and a hard spot. Mercedes knew she needed to talk to A'Lexus or A'saabi before she just called or showed up at home. So she tried A'saabi number again and this time she answered.

"Girl, your daddy and sister have been here looking for you. Why you get into these predicaments every time and end up putting me in this bullshit?" A'saabi yelled through the receiver.

"What you mean my dad and A'Lexus just left your house?" Mercedes said, sounding nervous and worried.

"Your daddy had A'Lexus to bring him over here to get you. He was furious when I told him that you got up early and left because you didn't want to wake him up to come and pick you up since A'Lexus forgot to come and get you," A'saabi said, thinking about what would happen if her father, Deacon Jones, found out she was lying to the Pastor. She knew it wasn't worth getting her allowance cut off because of some trifling shit Mercedes did and with that no good thug, Roc. But, she was her best friend and friends had their friends back, even in bullshit.

"A'saabi, how long have they been gone?" Mercedes said as she paced back and forth in the bedroom. Trying to make sure she had her lies together before she went home.

"About an hour ago because Pastor said he had to get ready for church."

"Good, if I wait another thirty minutes he will be long gone. He has to be at church for Sunday school, and then they go straight into prayer service before worship hour. So that will give me enough time to get home, change, and sneak in church acting like I've been there the entire time," Mercedes said into the telephone as she shook her head up and down, knowing she had her lie together. That's one thing she got from her daddy is being able to tell some convincing lies. Lies like the one's he told in the pulpit. With over thirty-five hundred members, many believed those lies because they came faithfully and paid dearly.

"A'saabi, girl you know you down for a sista and I love you for that. I hope you know I'm down for you as well. I really hate putting you in the middle of my drama, but I can't trust anybody else," Mercedes said almost in tears, but meant every word.

"Hey don't worry about it. You just get home safely, girl. Call me later to fill me in on what happened. That's if you can because you know Pastor Watson going to lay some hands on that ass. It ain't going to be no healing hands," A'saabi said, laughing because she knew this would be one time Pastor would not spare the rod, even though he spoiled the child.

"Don't you forget 'I'm GROWN' and I really don't have to put up with his preaching, praying, and pestering? I got a man that love me and if it get to that, I can move in with my boo," Mercedes spitted back in the phone because she knew that A'saabi was on the money about how her daddy would re-act if he knew she had stayed out all night with a man and worse, with a dope dealing thug having sex.

"Mercedes don't count on Roc to be there for you if it got to that. You know what he does for a living. You know hustling and praying is like oil and water. We all know that a hustler pray when shit hits the fan, but other than that the only time they see a church is when they're passing it to do a transaction," A'saabi said sounding hot about the way Mercedes praised Roc and his love for her.

"Hey, you shouldn't be talking about Roc because you really don't know him. He ain't like all the other hustlers. He's different." Mercedes said, defending her man.

"If you think he is all that. So be it. But, you need to listen to what your father is saying about hustlers, pimps and good for nothing men," A'saabi blurted back to Mercedes because she felt Mercedes really knew that Roc was good for nothing and he was a hustler who whored around on her, but she was living in denial and was going to defend her man at any cost. It was true that love was blind because she couldn't see that he was corrupt and meant her no good.

"A'saabi, girl we will be going back and forth over issues about me and my man. I have to get off this phone and head to the house of worship. But, best believe I will be praying for you because you're my girl. So, I'll holla back at you later tonight. Love ya." Mercedes hung up the phone and decided she just had to let her father know that she was a grown ass woman and needed to be treated that way. No more sneaking around, no more pretending to be a nice girl, and no more lies.

It would be a new day, a new beginning. She was finally going to act and do grown folk stuff with or without the approval of Pastor, and this would be something he has to learn to accept. He needed to understand he would have to accept the fact that she loved Roc and his hustling ways. He would have to accept the fact that she would be staying nights at Roc's house like lovers did. But, the main thing he would have to accept was the fact that she was fucking and she could do that because she was a grown ASS woman.

Chapter Three

The Way It Is

"Amen," Deacon Jones said as he ended the prayer service before the morning worship hour began.

Mercedes had to beg and plead Roc to join her at church, but she knew just how to get him to commit to going. She told him that if he could not be there with her to face her father after she had stayed all night and fucked his brains out, then she would have to call their relationship off. She made sure he knew that he couldn't use her truck to make his drug deliveries, and with her vehicle tied to Pastor Watson no cops stopped or questioned its location. She laid that guilt trip on him saying that if he loved her and was there for her, he wouldn't have a problem being with her when she needed him. But she knew exactly why she wanted him to go to church with her. That was part of her plan to piss her father off and prove to him that thugs do go to church and could love a preacher's daughter.

Mercedes had managed to bypass several of the church members that she knew would probably run back to Pastor before services and have him in an uproar. She and Roc found a seat in the back right hand corner of the church where it normally fills up fastest, right before Pastor exited the Pastor's study.   She knew as long as she could camouflage her and Roc's presence, the easier it would be for them to get through the services without any problems and she could build up her courage to face off with Pastor.

She hadn't been noticed yet, but when she was noticed, she knew it would be hell to pay.   But, it didn't matter anymore. She was in love and wanted to be there with her man full time. She felt that since she had graduated from high school, on her way to graduating from college, no babies, and no criminal record, she had the right to make her own decisions on how she should live her life. She felt she was grown enough to do what she wanted and with whomever she wanted.   She felt it was time that her father came to grips that she was getting older and had to make her own decisions about life.   It was something long overdue and much needed in her mind. And today was that day.

"Baby, how long we have to stay here. Because I have some business I need to be handling," Roc said as he leaned over closer and whispered to Mercedes. Feeling kinda out of place being he hadn't been in a church since his father's funeral fifteen years before. He didn't even feel comfortable going to his home boy's funerals. He always said that church was only for robbing the poor and having funerals. So, he stayed away from churches. He felt he had his share of church growing up because his mother made him go to Bible study during the week, Sunday school, worship service, and any programs after church every Sunday. He knew not to play sick because if he missed church service she would say 'if you're too sick to go to church, you're too sick to go outside and play.' So playing sick wasn't an option in his home.

"Baby, church last about three, maybe four hours at the max, but it go by fast," she responded back.

"Damn, baby you should have told me. I may have to leave before it's over because I have to meet my boy, King. I have some business I need to handle and it can't wait."

"First off you can't be cursing up in church and second you should have told me that you had to meet your boy. Like I told you before you need to prove to me that you down for me." She was irritated that he was making up excuses even before the services had started. But, she pretended to ignore his eagerness to bail out and just smiled as if everything was alright.

"Girl, you know that without a doubt. I told you before I love you," he said, but saying the 'I love you' part under his breath.

The only thing Roc loved was hustling and making that money. He vowed to never love a woman again. Lusting and leaving them was the only thing he was committed to doing when it involved a woman. He had been in a very committed relationship when he worked a nine to five, took care of home, and cherished his woman. Roc had come to a place where he wanted to settle down after she told him she was pregnant. Something he knew he needed to do because his father always ducked and dodge the opportunity to marry his mom and make their home stable. The relationship took a turn when ole girl got busted by her best friend after they had a falling out. Her best friend spilled everything on how Roc's baby momma had lied to him about being the father and that it was Craig's baby that ran the strip club off Cascade Road. The DNA came back and it was proven he wasn't the father of the child. This broke his heart and he vowed to never let another woman strip away his manhood. He became cold and callus when it came to letting down his guard to love a woman. So, he loved them and left them. But, Mercedes had something different, but he still kept his guard up, but not as high.

As Pastor Watson began his sermon he looked around at the congregation. He took in account of all the members that had joined the church in the last year and was pleased by the fact that he had managed to speak on subjects that kept them coming back. Most of them brought a family member, friend, neighbor or a co-worker. The membership was steadily growing and the tithes, offerings, and tokens of love offerings came in by the thousands. His church offerings normally totaled over forty-five thousand every Sunday, the tithes was well over one hundred thousand dollars. He had planned to extend the services to three services every Sunday and get a telecast program. He wanted to branch his services out to as many cities, states and countries as possible. The more viewers, the more money he brought in and that meant bigger and better things he purchased. He had penned over twelve books about many different subjects, plus he sold his sermons on CD's. He spoke and hosted many events that brought in extra money. He raked in big dollars from his extra-curricular activities outside from his preaching. So money wasn't an issue for him and his family.

"Members and friends, I stand before you today to bring you a lesson that the Lord has laid on my heart. He has given me this topic several times. I've wrestled with this because I kept saying it was not the right time. When the Lord gives me subjects to speak on I write them down, study the topic and try to apply it and if it is not the right time for my members to grasp the subject I put it off. But, like I said the Lord has been giving me this topic on several occasions. Today I feel that this is the right time to bring this subject to you," Pastor Watson said as he wiped his forehead with the handkerchief in his hand.

He flipped the page in his Bible. He looked around the church again and this time, he made eye contact with Roc. He just stared, not even noticing Mercedes. It was like he saw a ghost. He hesitated before he brought himself to speak, but instead of starting the sermon he asked the choir to sing a song. He took a seat to try and compose himself because guilt weighed heavy on his heart.

As he sat there pretending to be caught up in the singing he had a flashback to the days he's was living in the world and to see Roc brought back the memories he had with Roc's father. These weren't pleasant thoughts because the two of them lived a corrupt life and caused many problems for many families. His mind flashed quickly to the night Roc's father was killed and remembered he was the reason for his death. He remembered the heated argument, pulling the trigger and fleeing the scene. But, as he ran out the building he noticed that Roc about nine or ten was sitting in the backseat of his father car sound asleep. To see that innocent child and realizing that he would grow up without his father made him rethink what had happened. For a moment he wanted to call 911 for help, go back to perform CPR and try to say his life. But, during that time he was a ruthless unforgiving man and he just ran. Up to this date, nobody was arrested for the crime.

As the years passed Pastor Watson was slowly changing his life and tried to get out of the drug ring. He heard the rumors on the street that Roc had taken over his father's drug empire at the age of fourteen and was running things like his old man. Rumor on the streets also said Roc wanted to find the man that murdered his father and get revenge because of the financial strain it put on his mother to raise him. Pastor had many confrontations, drive by shootings with some of Roc's people and Roc sent a strong message to him to get out the game or get killed. As the years went by, Pastor knew he wasn't any competition for the young crew, so he found a new way of living and got into the church. He saw the mega churches pop up, the lavish lifestyles, and decided he could earn some quick money by just running his suave gift of gab and hustling.

As the choir ended their song Pastor stood and walked towards the podium to start his sermon. He cleared his throat and began. "Today's sermon is going to be on taking our young black men and streets back."

As Pastor scanned the congregation again he made eye contact with Roc, but Roc lowered his head to prevent any eye contact. He still hadn't noticed his daughter sitting next to the thug he had issues with back in the day. Apart of him was glad that Roc had decided to turn his life over to the Lord, but he cringed at the thought that he wanted to repent at his church. But, just maybe he had changed and wanted to turn his life over to God. Pastor Watson completed his sermon still not noticing Mercedes and Roc as being a couple. How could he have missed the two together when more than half of the church had seen it and shook their head in disgrace?

As Mercedes started to the front of the church to greet her father many eyes were on her and Roc. Many people took a quick glance and turned rather quickly before making any eye contact with Mercedes. But from the facial expression you could tell just what they thought, which wasn't very pleasant. But, that didn't shake Mercedes and what her plans were once she reached her father.

A few heard words said under some of the church member's breath made Mercedes want to stop in her track and speak her peace, but she stayed focused. Well until she got to Mrs. Lucy the oldest most outspoken church member in the church. Every church has that old lady that always say's what she wants to say without thinking she might be embarrassing or hurting someone feelings. She was the little old lady everyone just smiled at and over looked her unruly rude ways. People always saying she just set in her ways. But, today Mercedes had her mind made up that if she approached her with that foolishness she would politely put her in her place.

Just as Ms. Lucy was about to cross her path, another church member beaconed her to go to the dining area to handle a problem. She had earned the position as the Head Dining Security. She made sure everything ran smoothly and she loved the position because it gave her control. As she walked away, she managed to get close to Mercedes and in a soft whisper say, "Young lady, God doesn't like ugly and you doing some ugly things. Get your life together before it's too late." She threw in "God loves you and so do I." Before she rolled her eyes as she was entered the hall leading to the dining area.

"Whatever," Mercedes said nastily under her breath as she continued to where her father stood.

"Be nice, Mercedes. She didn't mean any harm," Roc said feeling rather bad the way Mercedes had disrespected that old lady. He may run the streets, but he still held on to his upbringing, especially when it came to respecting his elders.

"Hi, daddy," she said while holding Roc's hand very tight as she approached Pastor while he stood at the pulpit. As she stood in front of her father she leaned in and kissed Roc softly on the lips as if to taunt her father.

"Hello, honey," he said as he reached for her and brought her to his chest to give her a hug, but whispering in her ear. "I'll deal with you when we get home young lady."

"Daddy you need to deal with me now because I'm not coming home. I'm going to live with my man," she said as she grabbed Roc's arm and pulled him closer to her. Roc stood there trying to grasp the news hot off the press. He didn't have any idea what she was talking about and he knew damn well she couldn't come and live with him. He had too much going on to have her there on the regular. He loved living alone, he loved loving other women, and he loved his freedom. She would be cramping his lifestyle if she moved in with him.

"Mercedes, what in the HE—," Pastor blurted, but catching himself before he said something he would not be pleased at saying and regretted later. Being the pastor there were things you didn't do or say. And, church wasn't one of those places, especially right after church with members still in the congregation.

"We will deal with this at home Mercedes," he said as he looked at Roc with a look that said, 'how in the hell and why in the hell are you fucking with my daughter?'

"Daddy, like I said before, whatever you have to say you need to say it now because I'm leaving your house today," Mercedes said as she hugged on tighter to Roc, who wasn't saying a word. He was still in shock.

"Honey, tell daddy how you love me and want to take care of me. Tell him baby." She kept repeating, trying to get Roc to speak. He just stood as if he had seen a ghost.

"Mercedes, baby. I don't think you should be disrespecting your daddy this way and we haven't really talked about you moving in with me. This is all new to me. I just thought we were coming to church together and you were going home afterwards. I didn't have a clue, Pastor, and I do apologize," he said as he was releasing Mercedes hold on his arm and stepped back.

"What are you saying honey? Didn't you tell me you loved me and couldn't live without me? Didn't you tell me this baby?" Mercedes said with tears streaming down her face. She was hurt and embarrassed at the same time. How Roc could not defend her, tell her dad that he loved her and wanted to take care of her. Why?

"Listen Mercedes, you need to do what your father tells you to do. I'm not going to come between you and your father. He knows what is best for you and I'm not good for you. I'm going to leave the two of you to handle this matter. And Pastor Watson, I just want to tell you I enjoyed the service and hope to be back," he said as he turned and walked out the church. But, to Mercedes that was like having him walk right out of her life. Why he failed to support her and protect her from this wolf in sheep skin she couldn't understand his logic behind his actions.

"Mercedes this is what I've been trying to tell you all along. Thugs don't mean you NO good, baby girl. They just want you for what they can get and that is all baby girl. Use you, abuse you, and throw you away. Baby, I'm just trying to protect you from this cruel world." He knew she was hurt, but more so embarrassed and he didn't intend to lash out at her for her escapade with this thug. Well, not at that moment.

They were still in the church amongst his church members. They were the folk that supported their lavish lifestyle. He had a role to play and if he could be nominated for the Oscar he would win. So, Pastor tried to handle this situation in the best respectable way he possibly could do being that all of his church members were looking at him. Pastor never had to endure that type of disrespect and embarrassment in his church. And for his daughter to be the one doing it, made it hurt so badly. It was like pouring salt on an open wound.

All Pastor Watson wanted more was for his daughters to understand the that the members of   The Greater Miracles Church of God were the ones that afforded them the lavish home, the expensive cars, the name brand clothes and shoes, the regular hair and nail appointments, and the healthy allowances they received. Without the believers, there would be no church, no tithes, and offerings to continue to have these luxuries. So they better wise up and come to terms with the fact that they had to play the perfect preacher's daughters or it could all be gone. He felt that wasn't much to ask of them, especially when he was the one who did all the work.

Chapter Four

Sometimes Love Hurt

As A'Lexus entered the great room heading toward the kitchen after church, she noticed a sudden quietness about the house. Even though it was huge, there was always movement and noise. Being that they had two maids, a cook, a butler, and several yard workers, there was always someone moving about doing something. She turned on the seventy-five inch plasma television in the family room and entered the kitchen to fix her a quick snack to eat while she watched cribs on MTV. She loved to admire the nice homes her favorite stars had acquired. Even though they had a nice home it wasn't the same as watching them show off theirs.

She opened the refrigerator and just stood there trying to figure out just what it was she had a taste for, but she was startled by Mercedes storming in the back door.

"Hey sis, what up with you?" A'Lexus said as she placed the ham and sandwich bread on the counter.

"Your preacher dad is the problem. I'm so tired of this fake lifestyle 'til it is about to make me commit suicide," Mercedes said with tears in her eyes. Still upset at the fact that her dad tried to control her, and then Roc bounce on her after she had stood up to her daddy. She was hurt beyond hurt. The two men in her life had let her down.

"Well, you know that's nothing new about dad. Girl he was tripping this morning when you weren't home. He made me take him over to A'saabi so he could get you like you a lil' lost child. I tried to call, but nobody answered the phone. I'm sorry sis," A'Lexus said, feeling sorry that her sister endured that drama.

"Lex, this is not your problem. I just have to stand my ground and let dad know that I'm grown and he can't continue to treat me like a child. I'm going to go over to Roc's and find out why he didn't have my back today, knowing that I've taken chances to be with him many times. I've lied over and over just to spend time with him. On top of all this, I've given him my everything. I gave up my virginity to him, something I can never get back. And, to have him dis me when I was doing this so we didn't have to sneak and hide anymore." Mercedes said as she paced back and forth thinking about how she was going to handle this situation. She not only had Pastor to deal with, but Roc the man that had help cause most of the drama in her life.

"Mercedes, dad is one thing, but do you think it is worth going to Roc's after he fronted you like that? He's a no good dog and I've told you over and over if you keep petting that dog he would bite you sooner or later," A'Lexus said, knowing that Roc wouldn't be there for her sister no more than he was for his sister that had three babies, living on welfare, barely making ends meet while living in the projects.

"Girl, I love Roc and I just can't give up on what we have. I know he probably just did that to keep peace in church. He is just waiting on me to come over so he can explain why he did what he did today." Mercedes said trying to convince herself because A'Lexus didn't believe the lies.

"You know I love you and would do anything for you, but do you really want to be involved in that type of lifestyle. He lives the fast life Mercedes. Drugs and I mean plenty of drugs, there's guns, killings, the fear of being busted, and going to jail. Is this what you want out of life?" A'Lexus asked as she walked closer to her sister and looked her dead in the eyes. She really thought she could talk some sense into her and have her to change her mind.

"When you love somebody it doesn't matter because you vow to be down no matter what. It's for the good and bad, sickness and health. You have to be a ride or die chick for your man. I love him and I know he would not put me in harm's way." She reached over and picked up her cell phone hoping Roc had called or sent a text to explain why he ran out on her in the church. But, there were no missed calls or waiting text. A pain went through her heart because she loved him and thought he would have been concerned about her after the incident.

A'Lexus knew there wasn't much she could say on this matter because she knew that her sister loved her man. She knew the day Mercedes let Roc use her Range Rover to do a major drug deal he didn't respect her well-being. Because from that day forth, that was what he used to do his large transactions and a majority of the times she would drive him around. He knew Pastor had connections with the police department and they knew all the vehicles Pastor owned, so all the police officers knew to never harass or pull them over.

As they sat in the great room watching television and reminiscing, Pastor Watson bust in the room like he was the Feds. Turning off the television like they wasn't even there. Just inconsiderate and rude, but it was nothing any different than any other day when someone didn't do as he commanded. He felt it was his house, his rules, and his way.

"Mercedes Watson what in the hell do you think you were doing today?" he blurted out as he yanked his tie off, slung it on the couch, walked over to the refrigerator, and grabbed a bottled water.

"What do you mean?" she said with a nonchalant tone. Knowing exactly what he was talking about. But, she wanted him to say just what was on his mind.

"Young lady you know exactly what I'm talking about. Just prancing your lil' tail up in my church with that thug. Embarrassing this family," he said as he spread his nostrils, breathing hard and loud. Pastor eyes were fiery red, he had a bead of sweat on the tip of his nose and his fists were balled tightly close to his side. He was furious and he was demanding answers.

"Daddy like I told you before, I love Roc and I'm going to be with him, with our without your blessing. I'm grown and I can make my own decisions. You just gotta let me grow up, make my own choices, and mistakes," Mercedes said, not biting her tongue or looking in his direction. She refused to give him any eye contact because he always had a look that broke her from standing her ground with him. So, she continued to stare at the black screen on the television he so rudely cut off.

"Did you not hear that thug say he did not want to be with you that way? He ain't worth the time of day. All he wants from you is just what he has already gotten –sex. And you best believe you ain't the only piece of ass he has gotten," Pastor Watson said as he rolled his eyes and threw his arms up in the air. He thought, why me, Lord. "He doesn't mean you or anybody else he's using any good. He's the mistake you will come to regret young lady," he said as he walked towards her.

"Daddy you can say whatever you want but I know different. You think you have all the answers, you think just because you have over thirty-five hundred Jim Jones followers, you know everything. Well you don't. Roc loves me and he just said that to try and protect me from what he thought you might say or do," She said still not looking in his direction and holding back the tears that was on the verge of falling from her eyes and she refused to let him see her pain.

"Do you want to live with that thug knowing what he do and what the consequences could be for you? Do you want to be considered one of his whores? You know he will eventually have you doing just what he does for a living? Selling drugs, prostituting women and God only knows what other scandalous thing he's doing. Tell me do you want to throw away your future for that Mercedes? Look at everything I've accomplished and all that you have right here. It is all legal, baby girl. No running, ducking, and dodging. All you have to do is obey my rules and have just what you want without all that drama and worry." Pastor words sounded like he was preaching one of his Sunday sermons. But, he tried desperately to get his point across and hope she seen the danger in the relationship before it was too late.

"Daddy, like I said I'm grown and I love Roc. No matter what you say or do you can't stop me from loving him. Even if he does corrupt things, I know that you don't preach and spread the word for free. You use the sermon you preach to pimp folk out their hard earned money. So, what is the difference between Roc's money and your money? It is all corrupt," she said and thought he could say what he want, but he was not going to win that fight. She didn't know Pastor was so close to lashing a beating on her she would remember 'til she departed this earth. She was determined to make him realize she wasn't that little girl he could send to her room with just a stern look. She had grown up and it took more than just a look or some harsh words to make her obey.

"My job is to help folk not to harm them the way he's doing. He's killing folk with that stuff he sales. He is taking rent, food and utility money from homes. The users are struggling because of what he is doing to them. Innocent families have to deal with the drug problems he's caused in their family and community. It just doesn't stop with the user because stealing, killing, other community and family issues happen. Outsiders come to the communities to buy, rape, and steal as well. Somebody may be dying or already dead. Small innocent kids have lost their parents to drugs. Parent's dealing with the fear that their child will come to steal or even kill them if they can't get that fix. Mercedes, baby, you just don't know. You really don't know the problems that come with selling drugs, using drugs, and being involved with a drug dealer. That glitzy glamour life is only fool's gold. It's only short lived. All the money he has there's a very unpleasant story behind the mask as to how he has earned it." Pastor was full and he tried really hard to make her understand but she already had her mind made up. She was just like him stubborn.

"PASTOR Watson don't you stand there and say you helping folk when you have members in your church that could not afford to heat their homes this winter, but you still took their offerings and tithes. You have members that are in foreclosure and about to be on the street. But, we live up in a home with over fourteen unused rooms. You have members that don't have a way back and forth to work or having to patch up their cars every payday as well as trying to buy gas, pay insurance, and car note. But, you still pass the collection basket around, and then to top it all off you beg every Sunday talking about folk that don't pay won't be blessed. You have members that don't have lights or running water, living in shelters, under bridges, living in unhealthy situations. But, you can't help them, saying that you can't help everybody begging. They will never be blessed if you always got your hand out and your mouth open, begging. Instead of telling me what my man is doing wrong why you can't open your eyes to what you're doing to folk. You're no different from my man. He sale drugs and you preach lies. No different in my book." She had to prove to her little sister that you don't let people run over you and try to control you. She had to prove to be the big sister that would protect at any cost and Pastor just happened to be that person that would have to be taught that lesson.

A'Lexus looked on at the drama that unfolded and she knew her sister was trying to prove a point, but she also knew that Pastor was speaking truth. But, A'Lexus decided not to part her lips, but she was very attentive to what the both of them were lashing back and forth at each other. She was just glad to have her big sister stand up to their dad because she had come so close to this type of confrontation on many occasions.

"Mercedes you can get your shit and leave my house right fucking now. How dare you stand here and disrespect me in my house? You've crossed the line with me and you've shown me just how disrespectful you've become and I refuse to allow a child I've raised to stand in my home or anywhere for that matter and speak to me in that manner. I'm not going to accept it. You keep saying you're grown well grown folk take care of themselves in their own home. So, get all of your shit because this will be the last day you step foot in my home young lady." Pastor was furious. He had allowed her to speak far too long. He should have ended this long time ago. She had over stepped her boundaries with him. Plus, she had brought him to curse in a way he had given up years ago.

And as usual First Lady had resorted to their master bedroom. She never got caught up in the arguments he had with the girls. She knew the type of man she had married and he loved his money and refused to allow anybody to dictate to him on how he made a living and how he spent his money. So she kept quiet because she loved the lifestyle she had become accustomed to and wasn't about to let her spoiled devilish daughters ruin it for her. She loved them, but hated their conniving and scandalous ways. So, she always kept her distance when he laid down the rules.

"Daddy, you know you wrong for what you're saying. You just can't kick her out. What you think the members of your church are going to say? You need to be more open and understanding to our needs. This isn't fair and you know it," A'Lexus blurted out, not wanting her sister to have to leave the house. Well not to leave her home alone with their mean strict dad. She thought since she was the baby he would reconsider.

"A'Lexus, Mercedes brought this on herself. She chose to bring that thug to church to spike and embarrass me. She knew that MY church wasn't a place to be bringing that thug to worship," He said, trying to let her know he truly disapproved of Mercedes actions. He continued to speak his peace. "Mercedes A'liya Watson, my daughter coming in MY church and sitting there like I approve of the relationship. Not going to happen. The thug I've been preaching about every Sunday that's corrupting homes and cities. Do you know how little I felt standing up there while everybody was snickering and laughing at me? She could have done anything else, but not bring that thug up in my place of worship. She wasn't bringing him to turn his life over to the Lord but to come in there all hugged up like he was GOD," Pastor said as he walked toward the hallway, breathing heavy and with a frown that let you know he was hurt and frustrated with the entire ordeal. He needed to get some fresh air because he was beyond furious.

****

As Mercedes placed her last items in her Ralph Lauren luggage, she looked around the room with tears in her eyes because she knew she might be making a mistake. But she couldn't look at what if as part of the situation. She knew what she did was wrong but she had to stand her ground. She felt if she didn't do it her dad would be controlling her for the rest of her life. That was something she refused to let happen. It wasn't that she didn't love the Pastor, but she just didn't like the fact that she couldn't live her life the way she wanted. She felt as long as she was the preacher's daughter she would have to live the Holy Ghost way and she wasn't that type of girl. She liked the fast life. She liked to party to the wee hours of the morning, she like men with money be it legitimate or illegal as long as they had money, she loved fucking—even if out of wedlock. It didn't matter as long as she got fucked. She knew what she liked to do and what her father did for a living didn't go hand and hand. But, she felt that if she didn't live her life the way she wanted she would never be happy. He chose what he liked and he tried to force his way of living on them and it wasn't fair. He wanted to be a preacher and she didn't want to be a preacher's daughter. She put her last items in her bag and just stood there with tears in her eyes reminiscing over all the good times she shared with her little sister and how they would be missed. She knew she would miss her sister and prayed that A'Lexus could keep peace with their daddy 'til the day she left and went off to college.

Chapter Five

Cheating In the Next Room

Pastor had gotten up rather earlier than normal because he had a hectic schedule ahead of him. He showered, shaved, and got dressed. He wore a pair of black slacks, white shirt, and a paisley print tie in hues of burgundy and pink colors. Not the full suit attire he normally would wear when out doing church business. But, he still looked as if he had been dressed by a team of stylist. But, he and First Lady didn't need any stylist to dress or give them fashion tips because they had that on lock. On occasions First Lady would bring in her own hired makeup artist when they would be attending an upscale elite affair or hosting a banquet at their home. But, other than that she was able to dibble and dabble in doing the basic makeup, herself.

Pastor had a rather worried look on his face that caught the attention of A'Lexus as he passed her in the hallway as he was headed to his office. A look that said he was angry or he had been pissed off about something that needed immediate attention.

"Good morning, Pastor," she said as he breezed past her not even motioning to look her way or even part his lips to speak.

After he didn't respond she spoke again. "Good morning, father. How are you doing today?" That time she said it with a little attitude and bass in her tone.

"Good morning," he spoke, but never breaking his stride or looking her way. A'Lexus just shook her head because that wasn't something out of the ordinary. He was like that often. So, she was use to that type reaction and treatment. He was just a pastor that claimed he could rule the world, his family, and set out every day to prove that statement.

Entering his study in the east wing of the house he dialed Deacon Jones' cell phone number. Deacon Jones was Pastor's right hand man for many years and would give his own life if it meant it would spare the Pastor's. Deacon Jones loved his pastor and loved his job as head security at the church. Deacon Jones was a single father to his daughter A'saabi not by choice, but by the hands of another person. His wife Jessica had been murdered in a home invasion that went wrong.

Deacon Jones met his wife Jessica, while walking in Centennial Park in Downtown Atlanta. Jessica was a beautiful woman that stood about five feet six inches with soft curly mahogany brown hair and a smile that would melt anyone's heart. She sat on a bench reading an Ebony magazine minding her own business when Deacon Jones walked up and sat next to her. He had been watching her for the last two months and finally had built up enough nerves to approach her with a conversation.

Once he sat down, he lost all nerves and stuttered through the entire introduction. She was so soft spoken and kind that all that faded within five minutes into the conversation. They talked for an hour and during the conversation she told him she was going on four months pregnant, the father had abandoned her and her parents had put her out. Deacon Jones was already mesmerized by her beauty and he knew during that conversation that day without a doubt she would be his wife. They exchanged numbers, talked on the phone, and went out a couple of times before he proposed. They married three weeks before she gave birth to little A'saabi and he made a vow to himself that she would never have to know her real father and he would take full responsibility for her well-being.

When Jessica was murdered six days before A'saabi's second birthday, he knew he had to live up to the vow he had made about raising A'saabi. He would never tell his little girl the truth about him not being her biological father. Plus, he never knew the name of her biological father because the only information Jessica shared about him was that he was a big time drug dealer that was married and ended the affair after she told him she was carrying his child. Jessica family didn't even attend the funeral because they were still upset with her and the choices she made about deciding to keep the illegitimate child as they would call it. But, it didn't matter to him because he became her father at birth when he signed the birth certificate as the father. When Jessica died, his entire world came to a complete halt, but A'saabi's love for him kept him strong, and determined to survive the ordeal. He vowed to be the best father ever.

"Deacon this is Pastor Watson. How have things been going for you this wonderful morning?"

"Pastor, so far so good. Just blessed to be here and blessed to have such a loving Pastor, First Lady, and beautiful caring daughter." Deacon Jones knew just how to butter up his Pastor and put a smile on his face.

"I'm torn by some things that have taken place in my home and with my family. And you know I try my best to preach the word and live by the word. But, I can't have a child I'm raising to disrespect me, my home, my word, and my teaching of the Bible. I'm just not going to have it in my house," Pastor said as his blood began to rise and start to boil just from thinking about the entire incident.

"Pastor, you can't spare the rod and expect the child to behave. You know this generation of kids is uncontrollable and has an answer for everything we try to instill in them. But, I pray every night that the Lord will lay his hands on my child and rebuke that devil that might try to creep up in her. I pray Pastor that she continues to follow my rules and respect me. All praises go to the lord because as of this day I've been blessed," Deacon Jones said in the phone as if to be preaching a sermon to the Pastor.

"Yeah, Deacon I truly understand your request to the Lord. But, I know my own kids have gotten unruly and out of hand. Miss Mercedes has tested me for the last time and I asked her to leave my home. I can't have my child that I feed, cloth, and keep a roof over her head talk to me like I'm the hired help. I told her she had to get out last night," Pastor said, sounding as if he was unsure of his decision to put Mercedes out.

"Pastor I understand your decision and trust me if my child, A'saabi, would have done half of the things you've shared with me that Mercedes has done, she would be in the same situation. I'm not going to allow my child to control me or my home. I've done too much for this child that isn't biologically mine to have her disrespect me and think it is alright with me." Deacon Jones stuttered realizing he had let out the truth about him not being the biological father. But, he hoped Pastor was caught up in his issues he didn't hear his little slip up.

"Well, Deacon, I'm going to stick to my rules and hope she realize the streets isn't a place for a girl raised in the church. She will come begging my pardon once she gets a taste of those vicious cold streets. She just doesn't understand that I love her and want the best for her, but sometime we have to let them learn the hard way. But, we all know a rebellious soul have to repent eventually." The hurt could be seen in Pastor's eyes as well as the wrinkles displayed on his forehead. But, he wasn't giving in to her deceitful ways.

"Pastor, please do not beat yourself up for what has happened because I know and the church congregation know that you've been raising those girls the right way. They've strayed to the world way of living." Deacon Jones said trying to help the Pastor with his dilemma and not say the wrong thing to cause Pastor to question his friendship as well as his position on the Deacon's board.

Pastor listened, but still wasn't sure how this ordeal would pan out with his members. They had witnessed with their own eyes his daughter with that street thug. And then Mercedes was flaunting him around in church like he was Jesus. She had really tested the water with Pastor and she was going to pay dearly.

"Deacon how will the members take to all this drama and the fact that Mercedes is no longer living in my home. I know she's going to be parading in the streets with this low life. And it will only take Ms. Lucy to get wind of it and it will spread like a wild forest fire. We all know only ninety-nine percent of what she say isn't the truth" Pastor said worried about the faith of his church and the possibility of members leaving because of a disobedient child. A church he had built from only four members to its status now and to have it crumble by the actions of his devious daughter.

"Pastor, like you tell the congregation to 'Let Go and Let God.' Well this is the time for you to 'Let Go and Let God'. Stop worrying about all what's, why's, and should have. Just place it in the Lord's hand and let it be done. He will handle and deal with this matter." Deacon was really trying to get Pastor to see his logic on how to deal with the issue. Even though Deacon Jones did have a little concern about how the congregation would take to this news. But his main concern was making sure he believed what he was saying.

Lies & *Deceit*

It was just the affirmation Pastor was looking for because he beat himself up about how the congregation would react to his decision to put his daughter out. He knew that Deacon Jones would be the man to understand and support him in this matter. All he had to do was find a sermon to preach on Sunday to reel in his congregation to his belief on how he handled the matter.

In the middle of his conversation with Deacon Jones his other line started beeping, letting him know he had another caller. He removed the cell phone from his ear and looked down at the caller ID to only notice it was Sister Janay and it brought on a great big smile. She had been a church member for about a year and a half and had earned the position as the senior youth minister in a very short time period. Sister Janay was single, in her late thirties, no kids, owned her own Boutique in Downtown Buckhead and she was just a gorgeous woman from the inside out. She was the only woman in church that almost out dressed First Lady. Hands down she was physically more beautiful than First Lady.

A lot of the woman at church would huddle up in groups and breakdown her wardrobe, her hairstyle, and discuss her extra-curricular activities outside the church. Only a very few women church members would hold a conversation to just let her know what a great job she was doing with the kids and those women were usually the elderly members. All the others always found some type of fault with whatever she did in the church be it good, almost good or even great. But, this never changed her happiness about life. She would always speak and greet each member even those that turned their heads or pretended to be in a serious conversation. Pastor Watson liked her very well and sometimes it showed just a little bit too much. But, no one knew his true feelings but him.

"Deacon I hate to cut you off, but I have a very important call to take. I appreciate all the support you've given me and we will be talking very soon," he spoke rather fast because that was one call he refused to let hang up.

Clearing his throat and adjusting his tie he clicked over to the other line. "Hey baby, I thought you would never return my call. What took you so long?" He said in the receiver smiling from ear to ear.

"Honey, I got caught up with some paperwork and didn't see your missed call," she chimed in talking like she was First Lady.

"I've told you a thousand times you don't need a reason to call me. Whenever you need me I'm here for you," he said as he walked to the doorway to make sure neither First Lady nor A'Lexus had ventured down to his office.

"Honey, I was thinking maybe we can hook up a little bit earlier today because I need a few thousand dollars to purchase a few things for the summer. I seen a pair beautiful Louboutin shoes and a gorgeous Chanel handbag that I just have to buy today. Plus, I need to go to the beauty shop and nail shop as well."

"You know whatever you want it's yours. Maybe we can squeeze in sometime and meet at our favorite spot because

I've been yearning to make love to you," he said, wishing he could spend every minute of the day with her.

She said everything he wanted to hear and treated him like the king he wanted to be whenever they were together. Most of the late nights Pastor kept were locked up somewhere with Sister Janay making love to her until the wee hours of the morning.

"My schedule today is extremely booked and I don't see any free time except the few minutes we will get when you meet me off West Pace Ferry's Road when you drop off the eight thousand dollars."

"Baby I really need to see you. So, much is going on here at the house that I just need something to relax me. We don't have to spend a whole lot of time together just a little quickie to relieve all this stress," he said sounding like a puppy begging for a treat.

"I really don't see the time in my schedule today baby. I promise before the end of the week I will make it up to you because my body is aching to have you make love to me also. My body is missing the way you hold and caress me with your masculine tight arms. I'm missing your hot moist lips kissing my body and your hot warm tongue loving every inch of my hot steamy body. If I could I would baby. But, today is just not a good day and I don't want to rush our time together." Once again saying what Pastor wanted to hear. She had spread her charm and lies to get just what she wanted from him. He was totally aroused and it showed by the bulge that he had in his pants.

"Ok, baby I'll meet you in about two hours. Let me handle a few things here at the house and run to the bank. I love you Janay more than you would ever think." He was grinning from ear to ear. On many occasions he had entertained the thought of leaving First Lady many nights while lying in bed making love to a woman that he barely knew. He only knew what she told him and took that as being the truth.

Pastor disconnected the call and immediately found a lie to get out of the house without First Lady asking any questions as usual. He was really playing with fire and didn't even know that he was the one getting burned.

Chapter Six

What You Won't Do For Love

It was going on three weeks since Mercedes had moved in with Roc and she learned really quickly that what Pastor Watson told her about loving a thug was somewhat true. Roc had been nothing but a dog the entire time. She had witnessed firsthand the dirt he did to make a living. He often cursed her out for not running his packages as told. She had to earn her keep and he made that very clear on a daily basis. She would have to help with the weighing and packing. She did runs and on top of it she had to put up with his trifling ways. Something she had not seen the many times they were together prior to her moving in.

She hadn't been back to her parent's house since the day she left. She talked to A'Lexus every day to make sure that she was able to deal with all the drama at home. A'Lexus missed her sister so bad she often skipped meals. She missed them talking and doing things together. A week after leaving the house her father took the Range Rover and gave it to A'Lexus. He said if she wanted to live with that dope dealing thug let him supply her with transportation. So Roc gave her a 2013 Mercedes ClS550 black on black fully loaded to drive. But, it came with stipulations. She was told to never go to Pastor's house in his vehicle. Never get caught where she knew not to go and to always inform him of where she was going before she drove unless she was doing a run for him. She thought she had left the house of rules but it was no different at Roc's house. Only thing different they slept together.

Alexus made it her business to sneak by every other day to see her sister. She would go over to one of her friend's house and swap cars so that the Range Rover would never be spotted near Mercedes and Roc's. What her father didn't know wouldn't hurt him.

On several occasions while visiting Mercedes, Roc friend King would be over picking or dropping off supplies. Many times he would flirt with A'Lexus, but she was hard core and let him know she didn't want to be caught up in no drug drama. She would shut him down before he even got a chance to try to converse.

King was the next best thing to Billy Dee Williams, Denzel Washington, and Morris Chestnut. He was handsome, sexy, built, and had plenty of money. He stood about six feet five inches, a mocha latte warm brown complexion, a beautiful set of white teeth, thick curly black hair, and a neatly shadow trimmed beard. No visible tattoos was anywhere on his body. He dressed to impress every time you seen him and drove some of the hottest cars.

He flirted with A'Lexus every time she came around, but big sis Mercedes wasn't having him fucking with her baby sister. It was one thing for her to be caught up in the game, but to let her lil' sister get caught up was something different. Especially, not with the Don Juan-player-of-all-time players that has hurt so many women in the city. Even if he was drop dead gorgeous, filthy rich, and the most sought after bachelor she wouldn't let him get next to her sister.

Mercedes had cooked a gourmet Sunday dinner and who out of all the people to show up but King. The table was set with the finest china, the dinner consisted of baked ham, collard greens, mac n cheese, cornbread, and a double lemon soaked pound cake drizzled with lemon frosting with pecans. Mercedes was not doing much talking because most likely Roc was going to be a no show like he did before. A'saabi her best friend had come early to help with the preparation of the meal. Porsha and her date Tony had showed up about thirty minutes earlier and were being entertained by King.

Once A'Lexus entered the room King entire demeanor changed and he went hard with the mack game. He got up and walked up to her, giving her a LL Cool J sexy, lip licking look. A look that men think can win a woman over. Not true, only if you're LL Cool J.

"Hey, sexy put this change in your purse and get you something nice." King said as he slipped ten one hundred crisp dollars in the palm of her hand.

As fast as he placed the money in her hand A'Lexus blurted out "Keep your dope earning money in your pocket because I don't want or need any of it."

"Baby you going to turn down a thousand dollars? Don't you know what you can buy at the mall with that kind of money? Clothes, shoes, jewelry, and still have some money for later," King said, trying to cover his bruised feelings.

"What I need or want I can buy on my own. I don't need you or your dirty money," A'Lexus said with a stern tone. Letting King know she wasn't one of those street ghetto chicks he normally sweet talked.

King was his street name, but his real name was Clifford Jackson. He had acquired King because he controlled the streets of Atlanta. If he went to a club he always got the VIP royalty treatment. Valet parking, VIP area, top of the line bottles of liquor/champagne, and the best looking women in the club. All around the city he held lots of respect from everyone. He dealt drugs, but he always gave back to the communities he felt needed the extra help. He held a little arrogance about him, but it was a tolerable type of arrogance.

"So if you don't want my money can I take you out to dinner?" he asked, trying his damnest to win her over. He never encountered a woman who turned him down, especially the money he flaunted.

"You just don't get it. Are you slow or special? I don't want your money and I definitely don't want your friendship, companionship, or your meal," she said as she pushed her way past him.

She was cut from a totally different cloth than the other women he'd dealt with on the regular. It was a challenge for him and he refused to let her challenge his ability to be in control.

"Hey, sis, is dinner ready because a sister is starving?" A'Lexus asked as she entered the kitchen where Mercedes and A'saabi were preparing the last of the meal.

"Well, if somebody would have come earlier like they said, then everything would have been prepared and on the table," Mercedes said as she placed the ham on the dining room table.

"You know I had to lie and sneak out the holy house. Plus, I had to drive the Range Rover over here because I couldn't hook up with Tasha to change vehicles. So you know I had to drive all out my way, and then circle about three or four times to make sure none of the church members noticed me pulling in the driveway. Things a woman have to endure to have a peace of mind," A'Lexus said, laughing while placing the cornbread on the table.

As everyone sat down to eat Mercedes cell began to ring. The look on her face told the entire story. Roc wouldn't make the dinner again.

She excused herself from the table and walked into the hall because she knew the conversation wouldn't be pleasant.

"Baby, I apologize, but things didn't turn out the way I thought and I know I'm not going to be able to make your dinner," he said, but she knew he was lying because she could hear all the laughing and talking in the background like he was at one of his spots.

"You do this shit every time I plan something. You should be more considerate of me and what I'm trying to do for us." A tear dropped down her face as she spoke. She was angry, but she knew she had to keep her composure because she had guest in her home.

"Damn, baby you acting like I'm out in the streets fucking around. I'm out here trying to make this money to keep the bills paid," he snapped back through the receiver, trying to explain his case.

"But, you knew I had planned this dinner. They already feel like you don't spend enough quality time with me and that you're this horrible abuser. So can you just please come for a little while. I need you here baby." She pleaded with him because she didn't want to face her friends once again without her man. She'd received a lot of mouth from them about how Roc's just a dog and don't care for nobody but himself. She tried to prove them wrong, but once again Roc made her out to be a weak woman who believed her man lies.

"Listen, I'll do everything possible to make it up to you, but just let my boy King know I need to meet up with him as soon as possible so we can handle this business. Let him know he needs to cut it short and get with me ASAP. Love you babe." Before she could say anything she heard the dial tone. He hung up and had no intentions of trying to rectify the situation.

She stood there in disbelief. But, it hadn't been the first time he did that and she knew it wouldn't be the last time. The issue she had with him was that he never could be there when she planned events. She really thought moving in would make things better between them. But, as time went on things changed, he changed, and things went downhill. Through all the arguments, and him losing interest in her really made her want to prove that she could change him back to the Roc she first met. She loved Roc and would give her life for him, but she realized that he was just the no good man her father preached about on his pulpit.

It was one of the hardest things she had to do was to go once again tell her guest he wasn't coming. She straightened her clothes, wiped the tears from her eyes, and went back to the dining area with her guest.

As she sat down she caught a glimpse of A'saabi and A'Lexus face and she could tell they knew it was Roc with some more lies. As she looked over at Porsha she seen her smile at her and she knew even though they've done their dirt she was always supportive in her drama with Roc. Porsha never questioned why she stayed with him, why she put up with all the drama and issues. She was just a friend being a friend without prying. Her motto was 'you do you, I'll do me, and we'll be there for each other when needed.'

She hesitated before she began to speak because she knew all eyes were on her. "King, it was Roc he said he's tied up on a deal and need you to meet him in an hour to discuss some business." Mercedes tried her best to keep a happy face telling him that, but her heart had stopped beating. It was the fourth time he had done this mess. She was trying her best to keep her composure. She knew he was the one making sure everything functioned in their lives. So she knew that there would be moments, days, and nights like this in her life. But, why on the night she had her closest friends over for dinner again? The facial expression of her guest said it all about how they felt about Roc not being at the dinner.

Things between her and Roc had changed drastically. He came in at the wee hours of the morning, sleeping on the couch most of the time, sleeping 'til about noon to jump up, shower, and then leave. He always had one of his boys to drop by to pick up a package or leave something for him. It was just a revolving door. Never any privacy and the sex had ceased. Maybe once every other week, and then it was a quickie. No foreplay, kissing, or toys. There was no communication only if it related to the business or he was bitching about something that had not been done or done wrong.

Pastor was right when he said the grass looks greener on the other side until you get over there and realize all the maintenance you have to do to keep it green. He always said if you pull the weeds from your own grass and water it on the regular it will look the same as the other side. He would say don't rush so quickly to what looks good because it just might be the way the sun is shining on it to make it sparkle and when you get it you will see that it was the rusty spot that had a few drops of water that caught all the sun that gave off that sparkle.

Chapter Seven

Love Hurts Sometime

It was two weeks since the dinner and Mercedes needed to get out the house and the only place she could really go was to A'saabi's. Ever since she had stormed out Pastor's house Deacon Jones made some new rules for A'saabi. One of the rules was he didn't want her around Mercedes. But, this never happened because the two of them had constant contact. Each time A'saabi went to Mercedes she dropped her car off at the mall and was picked up by Mercedes. They always said where there was a will there most definitely was a way.

As Mercedes pulled the CLS550 in the parking space she turned up the volume to the radio. It blasted TI song Hello. She sang along because that song was singing to her situation. It said you would have some haters in the review mirror and to just wave hello. Since she had left Pastor's house and had not attended church in a while a majority of the members she use to have a relationship with ended their friendship with her. It hurt, but she realized that everyone that you think is your friend is just a person passing for that season.

Beep, Beep, Beep, the sound of A'saabi horn on her Audi was loud. "Come on before we get busted," she said as she rolled her tinted window back up.

As Mercedes got in the car she looked over at the mall and shook her head. This was the mall she spent a majority of her time and a majority of Pastor's money on the designer items she use to buy. Those days were long gone. Roc did give her an allowance, but it barely got the things she needed with just a little left over for maybe one thing she wanted to buy. The lavish living and spending was something in the past.

"A'Saabi, can we grab a sandwich before we go back to the house?"

"Sure, but you know we have to go through the drive thru."

As they pulled up to the drive thru window neither of them noticed First Lady black Bentley. She pulled up to the window to the right of them to place an order. When Mercedes noticed her mom she didn't know whether to duck or speak. It took her a moment to focus and get the nerve to speak. But, before she did, she made sure Pastor wasn't anywhere near or any church members close around. She knew that her mom wouldn't mention to Pastor that she seen her nor that she seen her with A'saabi, because she didn't want any more trouble at home with Pastor.

"Mom! It's Mercedes. How are you?" she yelled out the window.

First Lady looked shocked, but then it turned to a frustrated look. She starred for a moment, and then she pulled off. Mercedes first thought was maybe she didn't recognize her or maybe she just didn't hear her since they had the music turned up loud. So she asked A'saabi to pull up next to her.

As they pulled up next to the car A'saabi blew the horn and gestured for her to roll down the window. First Lady looked over towards the car and A'saabi yelled, "First Lady its A'saabi, Deacon's daughter from church." First lady rolled the window down half way, still with the frustrated look plastered on her face.

"Hi Mom. How are you?" Mercedes belted out from the passenger window.

There was a cold uncalculated pause, and finally First Lady spoke, "you know we're not to have contact with each other. Pastor has made it clear that 'you' made it clear that you wanted to be grown and own your own. So in order for me to keep peace at my home I have to abide by his rules for our house."

"But, Mom I'm your child. Can you turn away from your child just because Pastor said to do it?" Mercedes said as she began to tear up.

"Mercedes, you turned against your family and now that things are not like you thought you just want us to act as if nothing has happened. Do you really think we should just be that forgiving and let you come back to a home you tried to destroy?" First lady said in a soft whispering voice.

"Mom the home was already destroyed. So does the Bible teach Pastor to stay evil and or does it teach him to forgive?" Before Mercedes could finish talking First Lady drove off. She didn't say bye or give an explanation. "A'Saabi don't worry she won't tell Deacon. She's too afraid of Pastor." Mercedes said as she looked over at her friend and noticed the fear in her eyes. Mercedes didn't know whether to be embarrassed or to just be angry at the way her mom just acted. She'd always felt that her mom wanted to care about her and her sister, but it was Pastor that stood in the way of her showing some maternal love. Why he intimidated First Lady was only something she could answer, and she wouldn't be revealing that answer anytime soon. Knowing how fearful she was of Pastor, she would probably take that answer to the grave with her.

As they pulled into A'saabi's complex Alexus black Range Rover was parked in the parking lot. To both their confusion they didn't' know why because neither of them had spoken to A'Lexus any time during the day. As they exited their car A'Lexus exited the Range Rover and started running toward the two of them with a face full of tears.

"I'm so tired of his mess. I'm so tired of all the drama and living a life of lies. I can't take it anymore Mercedes. I just can't take it anymore. I'm never going back and I mean never. This is the last time Pastor will mistreat me." A'Lexus said as she leaned on her sister's shoulder and cried like a baby.

"What happened and what did he do to you?" Mercedes said as she tried to wipe away the tears and calm her sister down.

"It's just a combination of things over the course of years and I'm just sick and tired of it all. You know just how he acts and the way he treats us. He's vicious and conniving. He really thinks that God called him to preach. He's just a wolf in sheep skin. I hate him, Mercedes. I really hate him and his ugly ways," A'Lexus said, trembling and shaking with tears just streaming down her cheeks.

"Calm down Lexi. Calm down. It will be o.k. I promise it will be o.k.," A'Saabi said as she wrapped her arms around her best friend's sister. A'Saabi was always calm and collected. She was always considered the peace maker out of them all. But, with all the drama and issues her friends had they really needed counseling.

"A'Lexus calm down and tell me what he did. I need to know exactly what happened and if he put his hands on you, he will pay for it. It's one thing to say ugly evil things, but to lay your hands on someone because they don't agree with your way that's when I have a problem with you. I'm just as tired as you are over all this drama," Mercedes said as she hugged her sister tight to her chest as she tried to calm her down.

"Let's all just go inside the apartment and sort all this mess out." A'Saabi said as she reached in her purse and grabbed the keys. She often questioned herself as to why she kept putting herself in those predicaments with them. She felt they didn't appreciate the luxuries they had been afforded and the lifestyle they had chosen was going to take them through things no one would want to live through.

Once entering the apartment A'Lexus cell rang. Looking at the caller ID it was First Lady. There was a pause and a look on A'Lexus face that indicated she didn't want to talk to her mom. The cell kept ringing until she decided to answer.

"Hello," A'Lexus answered as she pushed the speaker button on the phone.

"A'Lexus, this is First Lady"

"Stop saying First Lady, you're our mother. Our MOTHER. Can you just let go of that phoney life for once and act like a mother?" A'Lexus yelled in the phone.

"I was calling to let you know Pastor is really upset at the way you've been acting and want you to straighten up, get back on track or else he will have to make some drastic changes. We both know he hate an unhappy home. So, let's not cause any more havoc and just do the right thing," she said in her soft proper tone not phased at all by A'Lexus rude tone.

"Drastic changes like what? I'm seventeen years old not seven, mother. Did you hear me? I'm seventeen almost eighteen, which makes me grown, mother. I'm grown enough to make my own decision about my life." A'Lexus yelled back through the receiver. She was shaking and crying as if she was having a seizure.

"A'Lexus the word grown isn't something for you to use so loosely, especially when you haven't finished school, you don't have a job, and Lord knows if it wasn't for Pastor taking care of you financially, we all know where you would be if you were on your own. Living like your sister in God knows what type of conditions." Still speaking in a soft lady like tone, she tried her best to get the message out without getting loud.

"Pastor, Pastor, Pastor! I'm so tired of hearing about what Pastor want, what Pastor going to do, and what Pastor don't want. Can you tell me what you want mother? Can you please for once tell me what you want?" A'Lexus asked, knowing First Lady had no answers for her questions; she was just doing what Pastor had told her to do.

The entire time during the conversation Mercedes and A'saabi sat quietly on the couch. It wasn't that Mercedes didn't want to say anything she really wanted to vent her frustration. But, she didn't want her mother to know she was there and cause more problems for her sister and best friend. So, she kept quiet, but it burnt her up not to say anything on what was said to A'Lexus.

Looking over at her best friend A'saabi she could see the fear in her eyes. Even though she was silent her body language gave off the appearance of a person fearing for their life. Mercedes knew if she even breathed hard enough for First Lady to hear her, she would surely call Deacon

Jones and let him know everything because with both her and A'Lexus on the war path, First Lady didn't know what to expect from them. This would be a time she would go running her mouth to save her butt. Mercedes definitely didn't want to get her best friend in trouble over some crazy issues she had with her parents. A'saabi was the kind of friend you could depend on at any given time. She always had her friend back even though she didn't agree on many things Mercedes did that wasn't right. Mercedes also knew if A'saabi was busted, Deacon Jones would make sure they wouldn't have any type of contact for a long time. Deacon Jones lived by the proverb of not sparing the rod, but he did slightly spoil the child.

A'Lexus waited for First Lady to respond, but there was a long pause before she heard her mother speak. "A'Lexus it seems as if you have your mind made up and there's nothing I can say or do to change your mind. You want to be grown like your sister and that is fine with me. I've tried to help you and I've bent over backwards by calling and letting you know what could get you back in good graces with your father. But, if you refuse to listen and abide that's all on you." Once again First Lady had avoided the question and done Pastors dirty work as ordered.

"Mother can you just please answer the damn question?" there was a brief silence, and then a dial tone. First lady hung up. Shocked and starring at the receiver in disbelief with tears in her eyes that her mother disconnected the call without even trying to answer the question. A'Lexus felt it was the last straw between them.

She tried to reach out to her mother and her mother out right shut her out again.

"The two of you heard it for yourself. She's so controlled by that man and his money that she doesn't care about her flesh and blood. She's throwing away loving us for a pair of expensive shoes, designer clothes, luxury cars, lavish home, and a bank account built on lies. How could a mother be so insensitive to her kids that she carried for nine months?" A'Lexus was baffled by all that had taken place. She loved her mother because she was her mother, but she hated how so uncaring her mother acted.

A'saabi wasn't sure what she should say to her best friend and try to bring some light to the situation. She knew what they were doing was wrong and that most of the issues stemmed from their behavior. She knew she had no room to mess up what Pastor was doing for her family. Pastor was very generous to Deacon Jones and if it wasn't for the salary her father made from the church she wouldn't be able to attend college for free, drive the fully loaded convertible Audi in the parking lot, the two-bedroom apartment that was fully furnished with no rent or utilities and a very nice weekly allowance. She knew if their actions continued they were headed for destruction. But, being their friend she knew she had to have their backs in secrecy. She was torn between what was right and what was wrong.

"Mercedes I know this is a bit much to ask, but can I come and stay for a couple of days until things blow over. I just need a few days to think about what I need to do concerning this situation," A'Lexus said hoping her sister understood she couldn't go back to that house because she would most likely say or do something she would regret.

"Don't worry sis I got you. Don't worry about a thing because one thing I do know is family supposed to be there for family. Trust me when I say through the good as well as the bad," Mercedes said as they both cried in each other's arms. Knowing that in spite of all the hurt they felt at this moment they both knew that First Lady did care, but just refused to open up and allow her motherly instinct to kick in to love and protect them.

Chapter Eight

Missing in Action

It was 2 a.m. and Pastor was still missing in action. First Lady knew with his position there would be many early mornings and plenty of late nights. But, that was a habit that was suspicious of wrong doing. Her first thought was to call and make sure he was alright. But, she knew if she pried, he would surely scold her as he had done on many other occasions. So, she put that thought out of her mind as fast as she had thought of it.

At first Pastor would leave out from home or the church office just as he was dressed. Being the Senior Pastor he always adorned himself in nice expensive suits, shoes, and jewelry on a daily basis. Always was a well groomed man at any given time. But, lately for his afternoon visits, he'd shower, trim his facial hair, and dress in a way that sent a message as if he was trying to impress someone of the opposite sex. He would spend extra time making sure everything was neat and orderly from head to toe. That was something First Lady thought to be rather odd. Because, he only went out to visit the sick, shut in, families that had lost a loved one or families suffering with an incurable condition and couldn't attend regular services. It wasn't like he was attending a board meeting or attending a seminar for the church and needed to shower after a long day's work.

As First Lady walked back towards the master bedroom after leaving the kitchen, she peaked out the large window in the living room that gave a great view of most of the front entrance. She checked to make sure everything was secure and that Pastor hadn't come in while she was taking her nightly shower. Observing the grounds she hadn't noticed any changes from the last time about an hour when she had last checked. She said a soft prayer that asked that he would watch over Pastor and bring him home safely. She entered the master bedroom laid across the California king master bed and starred at the ceiling.

Lying in bed First Lady's mind kept roaming back to what and why every other night Pastor had something so demanding that would take him from home for such long periods of time. She didn't want to consume her thoughts with it because she trusted her husband to be honest, loving, caring, and faithful. But, she kept resorting back to how things were when they first met and got married. As she lay in bed the home phone rang. Her heart stopped for a shear moment and the first thought was that something terribly wrong had happened to Pastor. Maybe a very bad car wreck or he had been robbed and killed. She rolled over and grabbed the receiver.

"Hello, the Watson's residence. How may I help you?" she spoke softly into the receiver, praying that it wasn't a call to give her bad news. There was silence with no background noise on the other end and it frightened her.

"Good morning. This is First Lady. How may I help you?"

Mercedes spoke up, "Good morning, mother. Is Pastor available?" Mercedes asked, knowing good and well he wasn't home. She remembered how things were from way back when she was six or seven and he would leave home for hours to only come back as if nothing was wrong. She remembered how her mother would pace the bedroom floor peeping out the windows looking for any sign of him. Once he came home, she would welcome him back as if nothing wrong had taken place. That type of activity with her father had gone on for years. As long as her mother accepted and allowed it, he wouldn't change. There were occasions when he came home and you could hear loud angry voices coming from their bedroom and sometimes the sound of people fighting, but once morning came everything seemed normal.

"Mercedes, your father is asleep and asked not to be disturbed," First Lady said in a low soft whispering voice like she would do if he was home. She feared everything she did around him. He was verbally, mentally, and sometime physically abusive behind the closed doors of their home. So she walked the straight and narrow at all times.

"Mother, if he's there go and wake him up. It's an emergency!" Mercedes yelled through the phone.

"Listen, young lady. This is your mother you're speaking to in that tone of voice. You may think you're grown and can talk to us any kind of way, but your sadly mistaken. You will respect me!"

Before First Lady finished her sentence, Mercedes cut her off right in the middle of trying to explain herself. "You know as well as me that he's not there and you better wake up before it's too late. He's been doing this staying out late for as long as I can remember. You should be tired of his controlling, lying, and abusive ways. He's destroying our family and he's the pastor that supposes to save lost souls and mend broken homes. Well he's broken our family in so many pieces that sometime I don't think it can be repaired. Mother do you want to live unhappy just to say you have a lavish home, luxury cars, designer clothes, and jewelry? Do you really want to sale your soul for material things?" Mercedes could hear her mother silently sobbing. She knew her mother hated Pastor's ways, but for the status, she dealt with all of the issues.

"Mercedes you don't know a damn thing about me and why I do the things I do." First Lady had never cursed, so Mercedes knew she had sparked a fire in her mother. Mercedes didn't know whether to take her mother's response as I'm tired of my lifestyle or I'm tired of you and your sister always butting into my life.

"Mother you know as well as me. Pastor is controlling, conniving, and conceited. So why go through with pretending as if he's the best thing that happened to you. He's a sheep in a wolf body. He's the wolf in the Little Red Robin Hood story." Mercedes was trying to get her mother to the point of admitting she was tired of being controlled and abused. She just wanted her mother to admit that she was at that point.

"Mercedes it's too early in the morning for you to be calling my home with this nonsense and I'm politely asking you to disconnect from this call right now." Her voice became cold and stern. She was at her breaking point with the girls and their deceptive ways. She felt they just wanted to be rebellious because they had it to easy all their lives. Everything given to them on a silver platter and she was tired of fighting a battle that wasn't going to be won. When she married Pastor and the church grew as large as it was, she vowed she would never allow another woman to come in and wreck her home. She refused to allow her own daughters destroy the lifestyle she yearned to have for years. She finally reaped the benefits and she would be damned to allow her two spoiled brats to ruin it all.

"So you're going to disconnect this call like you did with A'Lexus when she was at A'saabi house the other day? You know you're known to duck and dodge a situation that you need to deal with, but no you just disconnect, shut down, or run to your room. You've never been able to stand your ground. Always weak and allowing others to run over you. Mother, woman up and put your foot down. This is your life you're allowing to be controlled at the hands of a man that is cheating, abusing, and controlling you. I know you want to be free from this lifestyle to live your life happy and fulfilled." Mercedes was sobbing as she spoke to her mother because she knew if she didn't tell her mother that she was subjecting her livelihood to pain, nobody else would stand up and let her know that she really had choices in life.

First Lady's first reaction to what Mercedes said was kind of hard to accept, because she knew deep down it was true. When she was younger there wasn't much she would take off a man, never allowing a man to dictate how she should live, where she should go and most definitely what she should say. Earlier in the relationship there was a lot of partying, drinking, hanging out, but after things went sour Pastor made changes with how he handled his home life. The first thing he did was he laid down rules, took away privileges and had order in his home.

"Mother, are you still there?" Mercedes yelled through the phone because there had been silence for over a minute.

First lady was really hurt by the tone Mercedes had taken with her. She was speechless and she refused to allow her daughter to disrespect her in any kind of manner. So, she did as she always did, disconnected the call and sobbed silently as she lay on her bed.

As First Lady lay looking up at the ceiling allowing everything in that conversation to replay she realized that everything said was so true, and hurtful that she laid there and cried herself to sleep.

As the morning sun crept through the wooden plantation blinds she rolled over to notice that Pastor had slipped into the house and was lying next to her as if he had been home at a decent hour. He had been so quiet and sneaky with his arrival that she couldn't tell you the hour of morning that he had arrived. All she knew was he was home and that she shouldn't question him if she wanted to keep peace in their home.

Lies & Deceit

Pastor could smell the pancakes, bacon, and eggs as he was entering the kitchen door. Breakfast was spread across the kitchen island like old times. He noticed First Lady was dressed in a soft pink very sexy low cut short two piece lingerie set. It was like when they first met almost 25years before and how she always enticed him with a meal while wearing something sexy. As he reached over and grabbed a piece of bacon, he asked, "When was the last time you talked to the girls?"

His tone and the question startled her, making her jump. It put a little anger in her because she didn't want to talk about the girls or even get into a long drawn out conversation with him about what went on with them. She knew the minute they got on that conversation the mood would change. Her mission this morning was to make sure Pastor was fully sexually satisfied and exhausted. Because she knew the devil would be busy when Pastor had to be out late at night spreading the ministry with all type of single and even married women with intentions to feed him an apple from the garden. She wouldn't allow her wifely duties to go neglected so he could stray into the arms of another woman anymore.

First Lady knew she would have to lie to him because if she mentioned any sightings or any conversations with the girls, he would go into one of his long drawn out rages like he would do with the girls. Especially, when he's had a long day or gone overboard in spoiling them to have them lie or be caught not following his rules. With the girls out of the house she was the go to person to get chewed out.

So, she took the route that would lead her to hell if caught. "No, Pastor, I haven't heard or seen them since they've left. I guess they're doing well and don't need our help anymore." She prayed under her breath that he could not detect that she was lying.

"Well I guess I will call Deacon later to see if A'saabi has spoken to or seen them," Pastor said as he reached over to grab the mail off the kitchen counter.

First lady stomach churned at the mere thought of him calling Deacon Jones to question A'saabi. She prayed that A'saabi had taken a vow to never mention that she had seen her or had spoken to the girls. Because if she ever breathed a word about any of this to Deacon Jones it was sure as told to Pastor the first opportunity he got to run his mouth. She figured that A'saabi knew better and should keep her mouth shut if she knew what was good for her, especially if she wanted Deacon Jones to continue receiving the extra money she would slip in his pay to help out on unforeseen issues at home and to spend quality time with her. That was an extra few hundred dollars Pastor knew nothing about because she wanted to make sure he was able to do extra things with his daughter.

"Pastor, I want you to get your mind off the girls right now because I have a wonderful morning planned for just the two of us like old times," She said as she walked over to him and leaned in to kiss him. But he turned his head as if he wasn't interested. She reached over with both hands to hold his face close to hers and planted a kiss on his lips, moving one of her hands to his chest where she gently caressed as she slowly moved lower down his abdomen but he didn't respond. She felt a little hurt, but thought maybe he had so much on his mind that her foreplay was a bit much at that moment.

Moving her hand, he looked at her and spoke, "Tiffany, I'm rather tired and I have so much on my plate today that I really need to get started with my day." He knew very well for the last few months he was turned off by his wife's advances and plus he had just had a wild night with Janay, so sex was the last thing he wanted with her. The last couple of sexual encounters with his wife were nothing exciting, always the missionary way of having sex. Janay was a very adventurous woman when it came to love making. She had actually taught Pastor a few things and he did things he vowed he wouldn't partake in sexually when he was in the streets. But lately he was trying any and everything.

"Well, can we just get a quickie in to relieve some of the stress and possibly make your day go a little bit smoother. You know sex do relieve tension and put a little pep in your step?" She said, grinning at him.

"Let me get a rain check and I promise that you won't be disappointed," he said as he grabbed the toast off the plate next to him, the newspaper on the counter, and headed to his office." He didn't even thank her for the wonderful breakfast. He exited the room as if he had eaten a meal in a café and didn't owe anyone any type of appreciation.

First Lady was hurt because it had been several weeks since they made love and when they did he wasn't affectionate. It was just a one round quickie. No foreplay or cuddling. It was emotionless and effortless. Their sex life use to be full of foreplay, caressing and affection. She was always enticed by him and always felt emotionally fulfilled. Their sex life was an every now and then thing that she usually initiated. It lasted just as fast as it started. He never said sweet things to her like in the past and he never held her afterwards until they both fell asleep. She always felt empty afterwards. It had crossed her mind several times that Pastor might be having an affair, but it was quickly erased because he was so into his church duties that she felt he never had time for an affair.

As he exited the room in a hurry, she silently cried because she wanted her husband to love her again. She yearned to be like it once was, she hated that he didn't have the same passion for her like when they first met because she had sacrificed a lot being the First Lady. But she knew that when a man loses interest in a woman it takes hard work and sometimes a miracle to regain that passion. But she wasn't giving up on her marriage.

First Lady rarely socialized with any of the members outside of church and when they did have an affair at their home or church it was so structured that she never was able to invite some of the woman members to help plan the event. So, she basically was to herself most of the time. But, lately her thoughts were to start going out and spending some quality time with some of the lady church members since Pastor was always so consumed in his office most of the day.

Her first outing would be to contact Sister Janay the senior youth minister, Sister Karen the organist, and Sister

Jennifer the secretary, to see if they would like to have a ladies brunch. She chose those three ladies because they kept to themselves most of the time and didn't indulge in the water cooler drama from church. She felt with those ladies they could actually enjoy their time together without getting side tracked with all the gossip. She was nervous to do it, but she knew if she kept herself unoccupied in her home, she surely would go crazy.

Chapter Nine

Why You Want to Treat Me so Bad?

As A'Lexus entered through the garage door that led to the kitchen she heard the soft music of Usher played in the family room. She knew Mercedes was on a drug run for Roc down in Florida and wouldn't return until sometime later the next night. It was seven forty-five at night and Roc routine never had him home after twelve noon and never before midnight on any given day. The only other persons to have a key access and knew the security code to the alarm were King and A'saabi. A'saabi had accompanied Mercedes on the trip to Florida to get in some shopping so she knew it wasn't her in the family room. King normally didn't do visits when nobody wasn't home. He didn't want Roc accusing him of any missing drugs or money. So, he made sure his visits were announced. A'Lexus got a little nervous because she knew when she left earlier that morning she had turned everything off. Then she thought maybe Roc came home for a quick minute, turned on the stereo, and forgot to turn it off.

A'Lexus day had been very hectic and demanding. After finishing class at high school she had to go work a couple of hours at the hospital as an Admission Clerk. Even though she left Pastor's house she didn't give up on getting her high school diploma. She made a vow to herself that even with the unhealthy things going on around her wouldn't deter her from getting her education. Even if she tried to quit Mercedes was right there lecturing her on how important an education was in this lifetime. Plus, she knew in order to become the pediatrician she always dreamed of becoming required her to finish high school and go to college. In her mind there was nothing more important than her lifelong dream.

Walking into the family room she spotted Roc in the reclining chair with his eyes closed and swaying to the music. She startled him when she reached over and shook his shoulder. He jumped so hard it frightened her.

"What tha," he blurted out. The stare on his face gave a look as to be saying 'you scared the shit out of me."

"What are you doing home so early?" she asked, looking at him confused.

"I live here. I can come home when I get good and damn ready," he snapped back.

"Well, damn you, too," she smart mouthed back at him as she walked away.

"What the fuck does that supposed to mean," he said as a vein popped up on his forehead, showing he was pissed off.

"It means just what I said. Damn you and your funky attitude," she said, almost in tears.

Roc started laughing, which really pissed her off even more. The evil look he had didn't make it any better.

"Whatever Roc, I don't have the energy and time for your drama tonight. Save it for those thugs and my sister because they're the only ones that won't put you in your place." She was so pissed with everything. From the fact her mom was not supportive, from Pastor being so stubborn, for having to live under these conditions and to realize just maybe it wasn't worth trying to be grown and sassy.

"Oh you got jokes. I see why Pastor put your little sassy ass out," he said, grinning like it was funny.

"You need to speak what you know and not what you hear in the streets. Get it right. I left on my own and no I wasn't put out. There is a difference." He got under her skin when he started talking about Pastor and what he did and didn't do when it came to her and Mercedes leaving his house.

"Well it's the same damn thing to me. You left, you got put out, whatever, but when it all boils down your ass didn't have anywhere to go. So to me you got put out." He had a smirk on his face as he shook his head back and forth.

"Yeah, yeah, yeah. Can't nobody tell your simply ass anything because you always have to be right and with that I'm done talking to you. I'm going to get a shower because I don't need to entertain stupidity," she said as she turned and walked toward the hall to the bedroom. She couldn't believe for the life of her why her sister dealt with his simple ass.

It got under Rocs skin and he damn well wasn't going to let her prissy, sassy ass get away with talking to him in that disrespectful tone in his house. He would deal with her even if it pissed her, her sister, Pastor, and First Lady off, but she was getting dealt with tonight.

Entering the bedroom A'Lexus turned the radio on and began to take her clothes off so she could shower. As she grabbed her robe from the bed and began to put it on she felt someone breathing on her neck and rubbing her shoulder. Quickly turning around she starred Roc in the eyes. He had this hazy glare about him and he looked at her in a way that wasn't pleasing to her. She was a little frightened because she had never seen him act that way. Well really he wasn't home long enough to know how he acted.

"What the fuck are you doing? Get out now!" she screamed at him. She moved away from him, but he inched closer. Each time she moved away from his fondling hands he would rush back up to her.

"Roc, get the fuck out right now!" She said even louder, but he refused to leave. He was just staring at her grinning in a nasty tone.

"Lil girl, you know you been wanting me since the first day you moved in."

"You're crazy, Roc. You're drunk and high. So, get out now before you get hurt," she said as tears streamed down her face. She was afraid of him and she knew there was nobody there to help her.

"You don't have Pastor here to save you, you don't have your big sister to protect you, and you know damn well First Lady don't care what happens to you. So, come on and do as daddy say." Roc had turned into a monster. Grinning and talking with a slurred speech. He was acting as if he was high on some of his own shit.

Each time she moved he would rush up on her and start groping her while trying to kiss her. She was trying her best to get to the bedroom door so she could run out but he made sure he kept her turned so that she couldn't run far.

He finally managed to get her close to the bed. As soon as he got her close enough, he pushed her down on the bed with one hand and the other hand yanked at her robe. She tugged at the robe with one hand and the other hand she tried her best to fight him off. His hands were so strong and powerful as they groped at her robe and body, but she refused to give in to his demands without a fight.

A'Lexus was so frightened by his actions. She was a virgin and had intended to be one until she married her husband. Her mind was racing one hundred miles per hour. She couldn't let him take what she knew she could never get back. Her virginity, so she fought with all her strength.

"Roc, please stop. You know you shouldn't be doing this. You're high and you love my sister. This is wrong.

Please stop. Please. Don't do something you will come to regret later," she pleaded with him, hoping he would get up and leave. But, to no avail he was still groping and tugging at her robe.

With all his might he forced the robe out of her hand and pinned her down on the bed. He struggled to unzip his pants, as he pushed them down around his ankles. His penis was fully exposed and erect. He was breathing hard and heavy as he took one of his knees to pry her legs apart. His hands were groping her inner thighs while his mouth devoured her breast. He was acting like a wild animal. He was extremely rough and very physical with how he was taking advantage of her.

She could only cry because the weight of him had her penned down and she couldn't move. So many thoughts ran through her mind. She couldn't figure out what she did to make him want to rape her. What would her sister do or say when she found out. Her thoughts were jagged and she wondered how she could continue to live under the same roof her rapist slept every night. How, what and why questions just overloaded her thoughts.

Everything happened so fast and seemed so unreal to A'Lexus. She had become numb to his touching, heavy breathing, and gyrating hips. The entire time he was breathing the words 'I love you' over and over again as he sexually assaulted her body. Her stomach churned from the smell of his body scent. The touch of his hands rubbing all over her body made her cringe. The sound of his voice made her want to strangle him. But, she was helpless. The pain of his penis plunging inside of her caused her stomach to cramp. Her body was totally tensed and didn't respond to any of his sexual movements.

He rolled her over like a rag doll and violated the most private sensitive area of her body. As he entered her she let out a whine that gave her body goose pimples because it felt like someone taking a hot knife and cutting into her flesh without anesthesia. He pulled her arms down to her sides and pinned them with his knees as he rode her like he was on a mechanical bull. The pain was excruciating, but he didn't care. His mission was to prove a point.

His body tensed up, his eyes rolled in the back of his head; he let out a loud cry, and flopped down on top of her. She thought he had a heart attack and died. But, he rolled off her, and whispered, "If you ever tell anybody what happened tonight you will regret it for the rest of your life." He climbed out of the bed, pulled his pants up, zipped them, and exited the room as if nothing ever happened. He never looked back in the room as he left.

As she slowly rolled over hugging the covers next to her naked body she heard the front door open and then close. She knew he'd left when she heard the engine start and his tires peeling out the driveway in his BMW. The tears flooded her face as she got out of bed walking slowly towards the bathroom and never looking into the full length mirror that was on the adjacent wall to the bed. She refused to look at herself in the mirror because she felt violated. A'Lexus was distraught more because if her sister found out it would break her heart because she loved Roc in spite of his lying and conniving ways.

Entering the bathroom she reached over and turned the shower on full force and she made sure it was as hot as possible. As she climbed in, the heat from the hot water scorched her skin, but all she wanted was to erase any evidence of this horrible nightmare. Her mind was so far gone that she didn't feel the pain of the hot water pounding on her body.

A'Lexus had been in the shower well over an hour washing, scrubbing and re-washing her body as she cried. She felt as if she was on a deserted island. She felt lonely and helpless. She knew she couldn't go to Pastor because his words would be the usual 'I told you so.' First Lady wouldn't even entertain the conversation and most definitely wouldn't be understanding, and she surely couldn't go to Mercedes, the person that was always there in times of need. So, she was left to deal with this situation all alone.

She climbed out of the shower, dried her body slowly while thinking how nasty she felt. She dressed in some old jogging pants, a tee shirt, socks, and her sneakers. She walked over to the walk-in closet, reached in the corner and pulled out her baton she used when she was a majorette in her sophomore year of high school. She walked over to the window by the bed, peeped out to make sure Roc hadn't returned home while she was showering. She walked over to the loveseat in the sitting area of the bedroom, grabbed the thrower, a pillow and laid down, curling up in a fetal position underneath the cover as she placed the baton on her right side. If he returned home and tried anything else she planned to give him the worst ass whipping she could possible give anyone.

She had been lying on the loveseat for hours feeling she had done something so terribly wrong to cause him to act like a maniac. She was torn because he robbed her of her virginity. Something Pastor preached about as being sacred and should be kept until you were married to your husband sent from God. She lost her virginity to someone she didn't love, wasn't married to, and someone who didn't respect her as a human being. Not even as a woman. Her virginity was gone in the blink of an eye and she could never get it back. He took it from her because of his doggish, disrespectful ways.

****

A'Lexus hadn't realized it was morning until she rolled over on the loveseat and seen the sun peeking through the half shut wooden blinds. She tossed and turned all night long that she never remembered dozing off to sleep. The stench of Roc's body odor still lingered in the air. And the smell of it made her nauseous to her stomach. She still feared the thought of his presence and the anger was still harbored inside of her. Before it happened, she put up with his trifling ways because of her sisters love for him, but she hated everything about him.

She got up off the loveseat, walked over to the king size bed, stripped it of all its covers and tossed them in a garbage bag. Walked out to the garbage can by the garage and dumped them inside. She disinfected her bedroom and bathroom from top to bottom. As she was cleaning she heard the garage door open, but before she could get to the window the vehicle had already entered the garage. She prayed it wasn't Roc because she wasn't in the mood to see him alone. She hoped and prayed that Mercedes had come back earlier than planned.

"A'Lexus! A'Lexus! Mercedes yelled at the top of her voice as she entered the house. "Hey is anybody here?" she blurted out.

A'Lexus gave out a sigh of relief. "I'm in my room," A'Lexus said as she walked out into the hallway. She tried to act as normal as possible and hoped it didn't show that she was hurting. Her eyes were still red from crying and she knew her facial expression was far from happy.

As Mercedes walked down the hall, approaching her sister, A'Lexus could see she had a smile so wide and a very cheerful attitude. Seeing how happy her sister was it took everything in her to fake a smile, but she managed. "Hey sis, I missed you so much and I'm happy you're home," she said as she gave her a hug, knowing all along she just wanted to hold her, cry, and tell all the rotten dirty disgusting things Roc had done to her while she was away. But, it took everything in her to just hug her and pretend that everything was fine.

"Come out to the car and help me grab the bags. You know I can't go anywhere without getting my favorite BSF something," she said as she grabbed A'Lexus hand and pulled her behind her towards the garage.

"BSF, what the heck does that mean?" A'Lexus said as she tried her best to laugh and smile. The flashbacks consumed her thoughts and happiness.

"Best sister forever, crazy. You're my BSF and A'saabi is my BFF. Duh," Mercedes said as she popped open the trunk to expose tons of bags and boxes.

"Whatever," she said, managing to put on a fake smile.

"So how was this weekend without me?"

A'Lexus looked away from her sister and thought really heavy for a moment because she wanted to tell everything, but when she looked back at her sister and saw the glow in her eyes she just couldn't say a word. She knew she could never break her sister's heart.

"My same old usual routine. Nothing different," she said as she grabbed the last bag from the trunk of the car. Mercedes reached over and shut the trunk before they both entered the house.

"Well you're acting rather strange, not your usual self. Are you sure you're ok?" Mercedes said looking at her with a side eye.

But A'Lexus turned and pretended not to see the side eye, which meant something not right with what you're saying. "I'm good. I promise." She was burning inside and she didn't know how long she would be able to keep her composure.

"Well, if you say so. I'm burnt out and need to take a shower. Take any of the clothes, shoes, and jewelry you want I'm about to jump in the shower and take me a nap before you know who come busting in the house." That made A'Lexus skin crawl just to know he had to come back to the house where she had to sleep.

Hesitating, A'Lexus looked in her sister direction. "Mercedes can I ask you a question?"

"Sure," Mercedes replied as she started disrobing.

"If you found out Roc was cheating and sleeping with other women what would you do?" She really wanted to ask her what she would do if she found out Roc had raped her and taken her virginity.

The look on Mercedes face showed shock, but more concern as to why A'Lexus would be asking her that type of question. She hesitated, cleared her throat and looked awkward before responding, "I know he loves me and would never sleep with another woman. He's told me over and over that I'm all the woman that he needs."

"But," Before A'Lexus could respond she was cut off.

"There is no but. He's around a lot of women, many women throw themselves on him, but I trust him and I love him. Now end of discussion. I'm going to take my shower. Love you, sis." Mercedes said as she grabbed her robe and entered the bathroom to take her shower.

"Cool, take a shower and get a nap because I need to run to the library." She knew she wouldn't want to be in the house when he returned not knowing his state of mind. She just really needed to get a breather from all the drama and lied about having to go to the library.

Chapter Ten

Girlfriends

"Hello, Janay. This is First Lady. I hope I didn't catch you at an inopportune time."

Janay was shocked to be receiving a call from Pastor's wife. She thought their little secret had been unveiled. She hesitated for a few seconds because Pastor hadn't spoken a word to her that he had been questioned about their affair. "Hi, First Lady. How are you?"

"I'm doing wonderful and yourself?" First Lady spoke into the receiver in an upbeat tone.

Looking confused, Janay responded, "I'm doing wonderful myself and what would bring on a call from you today? I hope everything is going well with you and Pastor," she said, trying to pry and see if there had been an altercation about their affair.

"No Janay, Pastor and I are doing wonderful. We just came in from a lunch date."

Janay felt a lump form in her throat. It actually bothered her that her man was spending quality time with his wife. Hearing him always say that they weren't in the same place as when they first married. Or that he wasn't emotionally or sexually involved with First Lady anymore, always made her feel she had control. But, to hear First Lady confirm that they had a date and to hear the happiness in her voice, hurt her to the core. She didn't know whether to spill the beans or to hang up and call him. She played it off. "Wow, it sounds like you and Pastor had a great date." She waited anxiously for the response.

"Well, yes it was great. We went to a five star restaurant, he had me a dozen red roses and gave me a beautiful Chanel handbag. It was one of the limited bags that were only sold overseas. Only ten handbags were made and I was one of the lucky ladies to have been blessed to own one." First Lady gloated through the phone.

Janay was speechless. How could he go and purchase a limited edition bag when he had just given her money to buy a Chanel bag that wasn't limited. It hurt, but she tried to understand that he wasn't her man nor did he owe her anything. But, she felt slightly cheated and lied to about the entire relationship.

"Janay, are you still there?" First Lady asked after there was such a long pause from Janay.

"Yes, I'm still here. I had been working on some paper work for the boutique when you called and I was finishing placing the order for a shipment of items. I'm sorry, please forgive me."

"No problem. I won't continue to hold you, but my call was to see if you would like to attend a brunch with me and a few other lady church members tomorrow?"

"I really have so much I need to do around the store. I really can't, but I appreciate you asking." Janay was in no way going to be flaunting around with First Lady knowing she was having an affair with her husband. She could deal with seeing her in church because she felt that she could repent and be forgiven faster in the house of the lord. But, to start something she would soon regret wasn't a part of the way she made friends.

"Janay I'm not taking no as an answer. So tomorrow Sister Karen and Sister Jennifer will meet you about noon at Aja's down by Lenox. If you should be running late it's no problem. But, I do want to see you there."

"First Lady I really need to be at the Boutique handling some much needed paper work and putting out the new summer wear. I will take a rain check." She tried everything possible to get out of brunch.

"No problem. Once we finish lunch the ladies and I will come to the Boutique and assist you with the many things you need to get completed. So, it's a lunch date. See you then." Before Janay could open her mouth all she heard was the sound of a dial tone.

First Lady was excited and nervous that she had actually planned a ladies day out. She flung open her closet and started preparing her wardrobe for the big event. As she rambled through the many tightly hung clothes she smiled that she was finally going to try and live life to the fullest. She picked out a cream A-Line summer dress that always accented her shapely curves and a pair of cream and pink

Saint Laurent strap sandals, her Rolex watch, her brand new cream Chanel handbag, and her pearl Chanel jewelry to accent the attire.

"What has you so excited and bouncing around the room?" Pastor asked as he walked into the closet.

"A few of the ladies from church and me are having a brunch at Aja's tomorrow. I just thought maybe I should be doing more with my time since you've been so overly busy with things going on with the church after hours." Smiling and preparing her wardrobe as if she was going on a job interview.

Curiously Pastor asked because First Lady was showing too much excitement to just be going out to eat. "What ladies from church?"

"Sister Karen, Sister Jennifer, and Sister Janay."

Pastor froze at the sound of Janay's name. He knew there was only one Janay, but he asked anyway. "Youth Minister Janay?"

"Yes, why?"

"I was just asking because she had made a commitment to the church for tomorrow morning to work on a program for the youth ministry talent show. I may need to call her and make sure she remembered." This was his way of getting her on the phone to question her about this whole ordeal.

"No honey, she already had plans to do some much needed work at her boutique. I volunteered to help after the brunch, and then we can finish anything for the ministry afterwards.

Pastor got a little furious with the idea of First Lady taking it upon herself to mingle and change her daily routine. Her place was at home not ripping and running in the streets with single women. She was married and he felt married women and single women had no business socializing outside of the church. His take on the mixing of the two types of women only meant trouble. Single woman had no structure or respect for a married woman's duties to her family and home. He felt single women were single for one reason only and that was to continue to live life doing the worldly things.

"Tiffany I wish you would have consulted me before you went off making plans to entertain these single women. I do enough preaching in the church to give them a message of right and wrong. It's not your duty to meet with them to try and convenience them to take the vow of commitment. Maybe you should call and cancel for tomorrow." He tried his best to get her to see his point and have a change of heart. He knew if she started hanging out with these women eventually all his lies will come unraveled.

"Sorry honey, the date has been made and I've already made reservations for the restaurant." She placed the remaining items on the island in the middle of the walk-in closet and exited.

Pastor knew he had to go to his study to call Janay and talk her into not attending the luncheon. He knew once he demanded that she not attend it was a done deal. He knew if he told her he would cut her off financially she would cancel in a heartbeat.

Walking down the hall to the study he hit dial on his cell. The phone rung about three times before Janay picked up.

"Hello."

"What is this I hear about you meeting my wife tomorrow for lunch?"

"What part of lunch you don't comprehend?" she asked nonchalantly.

"What the hell is wrong with you and who in the hell do you think you're speaking to, Janay?" Pastor asked, sounding shocked that she had taken such a tone with him.

"I'm talking to your lying ass. I knew you were lying about not being emotionally or sexually tied to your wife." Her tone was hard and harsh, that of a scorned mistress.

"What are you talking about and I haven't lied to you?"

"First Lady told me you took her out on a lunch date with roses and gave her a new limited edition Chanel."

Pastor couldn't believe what he was hearing. He had always told First Lady that what happened under his roof stayed under his roof.   He was pissed that she was out spreading their business in the streets.

"Listen, it's not like it was told. We had a free meal that came with roses and the Chanel bag was a bag one of the church members brought back from an overseas trip the church helped sponsor. They knew how much First Lady liked purses so they gave it to me to give to her. Baby I would never lie to you. I love you too much to put you through lies." He felt he had sold a winning lie because not one time while he was talking did Janay interrupt him in the middle of explaining.

"Pastor if I find out you've been lying to me trust me you will regret the day you came up to me in church while your wife was only maybe fifteen feet away and whispered that you would give me the world. I'm not the desperate church woman you've probably been dealing with and telling lies. Trust and believe when I say, don't underestimate my kindness for a weakness." She meant every word she said and Pastor really didn't take well to her threat.

"Well, I will never have to regret the day I approached you. I've been sincere and I intend to be the best man you've ever been involved with. But, the only thing I'm asking of you right now is to call First Lady and cancel for tomorrow. We don't need this friendship thing to blossom because it's already set up for a disaster.

"Sorry Pastor, but I've already committed to the date and you know how I am about backing out of something. Don't worry it will go by without anything being revealed. Can you just trust me?"

"I understand you making a commitment but they can be broken. I wish you would sleep on this and change your mind. I do understand and trust you because you haven't let me down this far but I'm demanding you don't go."

"Whatever, just don't forget we have a date on Friday night and don't forget my token of love. I really need it to purchase a few more items for the boutique. I love you baby."

"Love you too." Pastor hit end on his cell and looked out the window in his office that faced the front lawn. The view was beautiful. He could see the home next to him and it made him smile. He thought if their home was big and gorgeous his had to be the same and that made him proud to have accomplished a great life. He turned off the light and headed back to the main house.

****

Pulling up to valet, First Lady noticed Sister Janay's black Mercedes pull up behind her silver Bentley. They both exited their cars and as they approached each other Janay's cell began to ring. She looked at the caller ID and noticed it was Pastor so she decided to release the call. From the valet parking until they reached their table, Pastor called twice and sent four text messages. All of which Janay declined to answer.

"Janay is there a problem?" It was very obvious to First Lady that it was someone she wasn't willing to speak with at that point because she fidgeted with her jewelry and dress before she responded.

"Oh, no everything is fine. It's just my assistant at the boutique. She always calls me constantly with questions," she said as she turned off the ringer and placed the phone in her purse.

"Well it could be an emergency. You may want to call and just check. It's always good to be safe than sorry. Just give her a call." First Lady had given an order and she expected it to be followed. She starred over at Janay as to be saying, do it now.

As Janay reached in her purse, the other two ladies walked up saving her from having to make that phone call. First Lady stood up to greet the woman when they reached the table. She hugged each of them and Janay did the same. As all the women sat, Janay excused herself to go to the ladies room. She needed to call Pastor, to tell him to stop blowing up her cell phone and if there was a problem to call his wife instead. But, First Lady was too enthralled in her ladies luncheon and conversation that she probably wouldn't have answered her cell.

Before Janay could reach the bathroom her cell was humming over and over. She clicked the answer button, and Pastor blurted out, "Why in the hell has it taken you so long to answer my call. I thought I told you to not attend that luncheon." Janay paused because she knew damn well he wasn't addressing her like she was one of his daughters. She became the angry black woman you see that has been fed up for years and finally lashes out. She loved the gifts, money, and lavish trips, but she wasn't in no way loving the way Pastor was acting about a damn luncheon.

"Hold up, Pastor. You need to come back correct with what you have to say to me. I'm not your child, I'm not your pet, and I'm damn sure not your wife. You can give orders to your wife and kids, so get that right. You're getting old and forgetful because last night I told you I was attending." She was pissed with the way he came off on her.

"Listen to me because I'm the one that make things possible in your life. Without me you can't flaunt and flash all the expensive items I've gotten you. So you damn well recognize and respect my wishes or..." He couldn't finish before Janay cut him off.

"Or what, Pastor? What, because I know damn well you're not going to let First Lady know you been sleeping with me and spending all the tithes and offerings on another woman. What are you going to do? Let me just give you a few words from the wise. I hold the triumph card in this relationship. If anybody is going to do anything it's me. Janay Renea Jones." Her face was tight and she meant every word she said to him.

"Don't you dare try to threaten me because you don't really know my position at the church or in the community? Don't you ever and I mean ever threaten me about what you will do to me! And, don't be late for our date tonight. I need you to see you."

"Whatever and I can't promise you I will have time to see you tonight because we didn't have a date scheduled. I need to get back to my luncheon." She hit the end button, put it on silent, and placed the cell phone back in her purse.

He was a controlling bastard in her book. But, she wasn't shaken by what he said. She knew she wouldn't be treated that way. He didn't even talk to First Lady that way and she would be damned if she'd allowed him to speak to her in any other tone but respectful.

She turned and looked in the mirror to see a woman that was beautiful beyond words, but scorned by her beauty. Her beauty brought many successful wealthy men in her life, but all she received from the endless relationships was hurt many lies and disrespect in the end. She knew she was worthy of a meaningful relationship that had a fairytale ending. Janay knew if she kept dealing with men in relationships and marriages she would become an old woman without a great story to tell in her old age.

Janay's grandmother had told her year's before when she was about sixteen that if you deal with men in relationships or marriages, you get lies, you lose your youthful years, you miss out on true love, you may end up having a child that has no connection to it's other family, not being able to see him when you want always on his terms and your left with a broken heart. She told her that in most relationships where one person is married all they tend to do is lie about being unhappy at home, about to leave when the time is right, waiting till the kids get old enough, always one lie after another. Before long you've wasted five to ten years dealing with crap and he's still at home with his family and you've aged, gone through issues, missed out on meeting your husband, and left trying to figure out what you did wrong for him to leave you. Never realizing he was never really with you. She told her that not only will she be hurting, but she's destroyed another's woman life, marriage and caused havoc in their kid's lives. She told Janay to never subject herself to the hurt and pain because she was the wife that got hurt and it wasn't a great feeling to have your family torn to pieces for life. The pain she endured she never wanted another woman to endure and especially not her granddaughter.

Back at the table, Sister Jennifer made a remark to Janay that she must have had to make a phone call to someone she didn't want anyone at the table to overhear. The comment didn't set well with Janay and she wanted to come back at her with a few words that weren't pleasant, but she ignored the comment. She redirected the conversation to discuss her upcoming Boutique event.

The brunch ended with Pastor calling First Lady to say that there was an emergency at the house and she needed to hurry home. She apologized to the ladies and asked Janay if she could get a rain check on helping her. Janay was relieved that Pastor came through for her because she didn't want to entertain the ladies any longer. They ended the luncheon with First Lady inviting them to on another brunch the following week.

Chapter Eleven
What's Done in the Dark Will Come to Light

Club Vanquish on Peachtree Street down near the Buckhead area was turnt up when Mercedes, A'saabi, Porsha, and A'Lexus entered. Some famous rapper was hosting a party in the VIP area and everyone from the A list was in attendance. Mercedes and her guest always received the valet, red carpet treatment because Roc and King held down the city. Once the bouncers noticed her in the crowd they made sure they gave her special treatment. They always received the best liquor and seating arrangements, too.

As they were escorted to their seats someone grabbed her arm. She turned to make eye contact with a very well dressed attractive young man. He gave a look as if he knew her, but she had no recollection of ever seeing him. So, she kept walking behind the bouncer that was leading them to their seats. A'saabi loved hanging out with her best friend, but she knew if Deacon Jones got just a tiny piece of news she was hanging out in the clubs he would cut her off completely. So, she made sure to only go out on occasions and to clubs she knew the church members that attended didn't know who she was or knew her father.

The club was really jumping and everyone was having a great time except, A'Lexus. She had been in a rather down mood, but she was the only person that knew the reason. As DJ kqu'en B from Chi-town changed up the music and had just about everyone on the dance floor, King pops up. His presence made A'Lexus want to throw up because she knew if he was there Roc was not too far behind. Sure enough before he could speak to everyone, Roc appeared. He went around hugging everyone, but when he got to A'Lexus he made sure he brought attention to them.

"Hey, my favorite sister-in-law," he said smirking as he spoke.

She pulled away when he reached over and grabbed her, trying to pull her close to him. "Roc please, do not touch me because I'm not in the mood." Everyone turned and took a quick glimpse in their direction. But, Roc yanked her closer, and whispered, "Don't you dare try to embarrass me. Get with the program and pretend that you like me." He snarled the words out like a dog wanting to attack someone trying to take their bowl of food.

A'Lexus pain went from zero to ninety nine in those two seconds. All she wanted was for him to turn her arms a loose and for him to leave the club. She had a thought even better and that was to get her things and leave. Once he released her arm he turned and told the waitress to bring the best liquor and beer to their area. A night in the club he could easily spend three or four thousand dollars.

Mercedes was so consumed in the music and people surrounding her she forgot she had a little sister. Two

Chainz's song came blasting through the speakers and everyone in the club went crazy. People started dancing right at their table because the dance floor became packed on the first beat of the song. Porsha was one of the best dancers in the group and poor A'saabi danced as if she had two left feet, but that didn't stop her from dancing.

Roc and King never took a seat in VIP during the early part of the night because they were too busy networking the room. Once they had consumed a couple of drinks, mingled with a few friends, and mouthed off about what ever new toy they had purchased, they eventually came back to VIP and partied with the crowd the rest of the night. Once they did come back, a majority of their buddies and a few groupies came and joined them. So, most of their conversations during the night was about who had the best whatever. A lot of bullshit talking and cutting up. Never, anything relevant about their life or what was happening in the real world. Many times, Mercedes made it known to the groupies that Roc was off limits. Most of the time Roc was flirting and disrespecting her right in her face because he felt that is was a part of a man's DNA and especially if you was caught up in the hustle game.

She had confronted him many times when they got home because she was embarrassed by his actions in the street. Several times she had stepped to the women, but Roc would always lay down the law that what he did with women was between him and that woman. He even made it clear that he wasn't committed to 'no' woman and just because they lived together did not make it a relationship. He always hurt her by the things he said and more so by the things he did out in public. She grew up being told that in a relationship there should be respect. But, she learned early that when you dealt with a man that was not ready for a commitment you had to either accept it, deal with a lot of drama, or you decide to get out of the toxic situation. You can't have your cake and eat it, too.

King approached A'Lexus several times while in the club to see if she needed anything. He was determined to win her over but lately his game wasn't working. Several times he had come by the house to bring her favorite dinner and dessert, he had gotten her several nice pieces of expensive jewelry, and he would leave a couple hundred dollars on her dresser. One time he had two dozen pink roses sent to the house and when she seen who they were from she tossed them in the trash. She wasn't giving him any type of idea that he could have her.

Not giving up, King leaned in as he was passing her, and said, "If it takes me forever to get you then I will have to wait until then. But, I know eventually you will stop trying to play hard and realize I'm a damn good man. I'm the man for you if you believe it or not."

She rolled her eyes and turned away. She knew he could give her the finer things in life, but she wasn't into thugs. She wanted a decent caring man that would respect a relationship. She knew he wasn't ready to turn in his player's card and give up the streets. It ran deep in his veins and a blood transfusion wouldn't solve his problems.

The music was loud and they stayed on the dance floor partying. Mercedes could see out the corner of her eye that Roc was with some groupie exchanging numbers. Porsha leaned over and whispered, "hey, your man over in the cut with some chick. You need to go over and check him."

"Girl, it's probably some type of business transaction." She mouthed off because she knew his conversation with that girl wasn't anything dealing with business but she refused to let her friends know exactly how she felt. In situations like this she just kept a deaf ear and a blind eye to what was going on with him.

The girls all decided to go over to the ladies room, but on the way there the same guy that grabbed Mercedes arm was standing by the hall entrance. As she approached him he moved over to block the entrance.

"Excuse me, but can we get through," Porsha mouthed off because she knew he seen them coming, and then she was pissed because he was blocking the entrance to the ladies bathroom when the men's was in the opposite direction. She thought what the fuck up with his dumb ass?

He stood there not moving, just staring at Mercedes as if she had placed a spell on him. "What the fuck wrong with your dumb ass?" Porsha asked as she tried to push him away from the entrance. He was stiff as a wall and didn't crack a smile or say a word. He just kept starring at Mercedes.

"Why in the hell are you starring at my friend? You pervert. Get the fuck out the way before I fuck you up." Porsha was pissed off. She wasn't about to let him stand there and act like an asshole. As she pushed him again, she got very close in his face with direct eye contact, and asked, "why the hell all the damn good looking mutha fuckers have to be gay, dumb, slow, or with a trifling bitch? It's always something about the cute ones. They're always the ones to be fucked up." She said as she pushed past him and waved at the other girls to pass through.

"Girl, let's just go to the other bathroom across the club because I'm not in the mood for this simple shit," Mercedes said as she began to turn and walk away.

But, before she could turn around to leave, old dude finally had something to say. "So you don't remember me, Mercedes?" he said in a very strong tone.

Snapping back with an attitude she responded back. "Are you talking to me?"

"Yes, Mercedes. I'm talking to you. Who else would I be speaking to?"

"Well I wouldn't know because I don't know who you know. She smart mouthed back to him.

"Think back to your freshman year at Spelman in your dorm room one late Friday night after a game?"

It still didn't ring a bell because that was a couple of years prior and so much had happened since then. Plus it was her freshman year, and a hell of a lot went on back then.

"No, I'm not sure what you're referring to and maybe you have the wrong person."

"No, no. You're the right person and you remember exactly who I am."

Mercedes still tried to jog her memory. She asked him to move from the entrance so her friends could go into the ladies room and they could talk. She made sure she was hidden in the corner out of the view of Roc and King. She knew if Roc spotted her talking to a man or anyone outside their group of VIP guest, it wouldn't be nice.

"So what is on your mind that is occupying me from having a good time?"

"I'm your freshman year roommate brother. Does that ring a bell?" He asked as he reached over to try and touch her breast.

"What the fuck are you doing? Keep your hands to yourself, please," she said as she slapped at his hand. Looking at him and thinking, this young boy must be some kind of crazy perverted maniac. She was under the influence so what he said about her freshman roommate didn't register and by this time the girls were coming out of the ladies room.

As they began to walk back towards the VIP area this lil' pervert walks up behind Mercedes and whisper "I know you miss me. Don't pretend that you don't know me because you performed oral sex on me on my sixteenth birthday." Her eyes widen and she looked stunned because it was all coming back to her. He had come to the dorm to see his sister, but she was out on the town.

Mercedes had been drinking and seeing this stud young boy that was hitting on her, turned her on and one thing lead to another. She turned to confront him, but by this time Roc had come to see what had taken them so long.

"Damn, baby. I thought you left the building or you had bladder problems." Grabbing her hand and pulling her close to him after he peeped out the pervert watching his woman. "Are you ok, baby?" He said trying to man up. Even though he flirted and got numbers in the club, he kept all eyes off Mercedes and made sure he let the fella's in the club know she was off limits.

"Yeah, I'm fine we were just laughing, talking, a freshening up, and lost track of how long we were in the restroom. You know how ladies do when they all get together." Taking her left hand, reaching up to turn Rocs face towards her as she planted a kiss on his lips. The lil' fellow looked and walked away. Her guess was he had gotten the picture she had a man.

As they returned to VIP, a ratchet, disrespectful chick walks up and grabs Roc's arm, pulling him away from Mercedes hold she had on his arm. Mercedes was startled because she was a little under the influence and didn't really notice the girl walking up to Roc. She was some random chick in the club that thought just because she lived in East Atlanta she could do some shit like that with her man.

"Excuse me!" Mercedes blurted as she stared at the chick.

"You're excused," The chick said as she leaned over and kissed Roc on the cheek.

Mercedes facial expression showed her thoughts. She thought, oh hell naw this bitch didn't. She looked at Roc who seemed comfortable with the kiss. "Bitch, you don't know me and your surely don't know he's off limits. So, I suggest you get your paws off him before I beat that ass."

"Roc, you better tell your little groupie to step off because I'm not in the mood for no fighting a bitch tonight."

"Groupie! Bitch! No you didn't just call me a groupie and a bitch Roc you better let this random chick know before I have to show her ass a thing or two." Mercedes had her fist balled up close to her sides just waiting for her to say another word. There were many things Mercedes just allowed to roll off her back, but being called a bitch wasn't one. And, to disrespect her in front of her man, her friends, and then in the club, that was the ultimate no, no, in her book.

"Calm your ass down, Mercedes. Stop making a scene in the club like some alley hood chick."

Mercedes stood there in disbelief because Roc was telling her to calm down instead of checking this random ass chick that disrespected her. "Roc, you telling me to calm down but this 'Ran-dumb' ass bitch just waltz up to you and kiss you like its ok? What the fuck I suppose to do?"

As she stood there waiting on an answer Porsha grabbed her arm and tried to pull her away, but she wasn't leaving without an answer. "So what am I supposed to do, Roc?" She yelled at him.

"Get your ass back to our VIP area and wait until I get there." He gave Mercedes a quick look and grabbed the chick arm pulling her behind him as he walked through the crowd.

A'Lexus and A'saabi looked on in shock because this happened nine out of ten times they've been in the club. There's always some chick hanging on to Roc's arm or he's in one of the cut's rubbing and kissing on a woman. And every time Mercedes said something he lashed out at her and she would do as she was told- to either go back to VIP or get her shit and leave. They learned early in the party life that Mercedes seen just as much as them and accepted it so there was nothing for them to do about what she accepted.

They all returned to VIP and partied until the wee hours of the morning. Mercedes had blown off the incident and was partying as if nothing happened. A'Lexus was still in her down and out mood, but she did have a few drinks. A'saabi left around midnight. Even though she lived on her own, she still acted as if she lived with Deacon Jones and had a curfew. Porsha was always a ride or die chick and hung until they turned the lights on in the club. King had gotten a call and Roc rode out with him. Those two were thick as thieves and always into something. But, one thing about it they had each other's back.

Chapter Twelve

Scorned

Janay hadn't been to church in about two weeks. She got fed up from all the lies that Pastor told. The last time they were together, she questioned him about the new vehicle First Lady drove. He came up with a lie that she purchased it with her own money and he didn't control what she did with it. Janay knew that was a lie because First Lady bragged to all the ladies at their ladies day out on how he bought her expensive gifts. Plus, she did a tag search with the motor vehicle department and the tag was registered to Franklin Watson. First Lady's name was nowhere on the title of the car. She got fed up with the lying and to top things off, today was another First Lady luncheon. She had debated about attending, but she wanted to hear the latest on what Pastor had purchased. It was always something flirty, flashy and expensive.

She already had her attire spread out cross the California king bed. She decided on a silhouette Michael Kors form fitting, soft blush pink dress. The dressed accented every curve and her full breast. She took out her Michael Kors jewelry and a pair of Michael Kors pumps. She didn't want to overdo it and she most definitely didn't want to under dress for any occasion with First Lady.

Dressing wasn't an issue with her, but whenever she was around First Lady she wanted to impress her with what she knew about fashion.

She started her routine ritual of getting dress, which normally took well over two hours. She always started with a nice warm soaking of about twelve to fifteen minutes and a minute longer her body would start to wrinkle and she looked like she aged two years. She towel pat her body dry because she felt it left in the moisture and not cause her skin to get dry looking. Before she would put any clothing on she would allow five minutes for her body to completely dry. While that time passed, she drank an eight ounce glass of room temperature water to lock her body temperature. The next step would be to put on her undergarments, do her makeup, put on her body lotion, touch up her nails, toes, put on her shoes, comb her hair, and slip on her dress. She looked at herself in different angles in the mirror to make sure she looked her best.

****

First Lady had circled the parking lot a couple of times before parking her brand new 2013 Maserati in a reserved parking spot right in front of the restaurant. A parking spot where from any seat in the restaurant it could be seen at all angles. The car was fully loaded with all the bells and whistles. Navigational system that talked to you, rear back up cameras, ostrich hand sewn leather heated vibrating seats that contoured to your body's shape, top of the line mahogany wood, and twelve Boise surround sound speakers in the head rest, door panels, and dashboard. It was one of the top of the line luxury vehicles that turned many heads.

Once First Lady took her seat it didn't take her a second to chime in about her new gift from Pastor. She expressed how lucky she was to have such a loving and caring man. She often bragged on him in many conversations. Janay got a little burnt out, hearing about how wonderful Pastor was and how he catered to her every wish. Because from the stories Pastor was telling her, First Lady was living on prayers because he was ready to file for a divorce. The only reason he didn't file because he feared the church members would vote him out of his own church or his membership would decline.

"Ladies I must say I'm totally blessed to have one of the most giving, caring, and God fearing husbands. I've prayed many prayers and had the faith of a mustard seed when I prayed for my soul mate. I'm here to say if you ask, you most certainly will receive. If you believe without a doubt," First Lady said as she reached over and patted Sister Janay's left knee. Janay gave a slight smile, but she wanted to ask why the hell she was touching her knee. But, she didn't need to ask because First Lady answered her question.

"Ladies if you to just pray for your soul mate, God to will answer your prayers the same as he did for me." Looking at each lady as if she was trying to convince them that what she said was the truth. Each of the ladies gave a half smirk smile and let her continue. "You need to be specific in what you're asking for in a mate. Be as specific as possible when describing to God your future mate's physical, mental, social, spiritual, and financial statuses. You have to tell God what your heart desires are ladies." Janay really wanted to punch her in the mouth in order to shut her up. She didn't need her giving a lecture on how to get a man or keeping one. Janay never had an issue with getting a man, especially other women's men. That wasn't the problem. The problem was getting a single man ready for a committed relationship.

Janay so rudely interrupted First Lady by asking a question that she knew would shock everyone sitting at the table. "So First Lady, you brag on Pastor all the time. Does he do the same when he's out?" Everyone turned and starred waiting on her to respond. Janay made eye contact as if she was deaf and needed to read her lips.

"Janay, honey, I don't need to wonder if Pastor is doing the same because when it all boils down, I'm the one with the key and deeds to the luxury home. I'm the one with the title and driving the expensive cars. I'm the one he comes home to each and every night. I'm the one on the bank accounts. So, why should I be worrying if he does or not," First Lady asked as she took a sip of her sweet tea, not feeling a bit embarrassed by Janay's question. That was one thing about her; she was always gracious and showed total control in any situation, even if the intent was to embarrass her.

"So you don't worry just a little about the late nights? Because there are only so much church activities you can be doing late at night." Janay really tried to push some buttons and get First Lady pissed. But, First Lady remained composed and continued eating her meal.

"No, never because what is done in the dark will surely come to light. I pray every time he leaves home. I pray that he's safe, he does God's work, and if he's doing anything that is unsightly in Gods eyes he will come to his senses and change his ways. You see time brings about change and all we have to do is pray for it." The ladies shook their heads in agreement, all but Janay. She wasn't buying First Lady's Ms. Goody two shoes attitude. She knew deep down, there were some lies told, a hurting heart, and plenty of deceitful ways. But, it was just a matter of time before someone couldn't take it anymore and everything would hit the fan.

Janay was pissed with First Lady for playing like she had a happy home, but really it was her own insecurities about what she did wrong. The bragging and boasting sparked a fire in her. She knew she should be upset with Pastor, but her angry emotions were all tied to First Lady. She could deal with the fact that they were married, but she wanted her to leave it at just being married. Not all the extras she mentioned. The jealousy was really about her not having her own man. A man she didn't have to share. She wanted the lavish luxurious lifestyle that every woman dreamed of. But, she was stuck with no kids, an average job, and another woman's man. Janay felt if she could make First Lady's life miserable just maybe it would take some of the hatred she had away. That innocent nice lady that first came to Greater Miracle Church of God changed. She started to allow bitterness and jealousy take control of her emotions.

Sister Karen noticed the conversation going sour and decided to change the subject before any drama started. "So, First Lady, we need to plan a females retreat. We need to start thinking about a place that's rejuvenating to our mind, body, and souls. An Empowerment weekend and invite other females from our parent and sister churches in the state. We could do seminars, health checks, beauty makeovers, financial advice, and other booths that would teach woman the necessities of maintaining a substantial fulfilled life.

"Yes, that sounds great, Karen," Sister Jennifer said while taking out a pen and paper from her purse to jot down some notes. First Lady nodding her head in agreement. But Janay sat there rolling her eyes not saying a word. She was pissed beyond pissed.

The ladies wrapped up another luncheon and decided to get together in a few days so they could go over plans to host the female retreat. All the ladies hugged and walked out the restaurant to their cars. Janay was the only person that had parked further out in the parking lot. The other ladies offered her a ride, but she declined.

As Janay walked to the parking lot she noticed what she thought was Pastors car in the adjacent parking deck. She focused in to make sure it was his 2013 silver Porsche Panamera. She spotted the personalized tag that read: icansavu. As she continued to walk she noticed this man and woman walking all snuggled up next to each other as if it was freezing outside, but the weather was well in the ninety's. She heard a husky laugh that sounded so familiar, but continued to walk towards her car.

As she opened her driver's door it hit her that the laugh was that of Pastor Watson's. He had a very distinguished laugh that you knew before he was seen. Janay got in her car, but starred out her front windshield, noticing that the man had leaned the woman back on the hood as he kissed her passionately. The longer she starred the more focused her vision became and she noticed that it was Pastor and Deacon Jones daughter A'saabi. She was in total shock. Just flabbergasted by what she saw. Her first thought was to drive up and confront him, but then she realized she was just his mistress, the other scandalous, home-wrecker, who didn't have a pot to piss in even if she bought the pot with her own money. She felt helpless, hurt, and scorned by what she saw Pastor doing and it hurt. She wanted to cry, but could only laugh at the fact that he was playing her because from the look of things, she wasn't the only mistress. She couldn't believe her eyes and the fact that he took advantage of an innocent child. The entire, time she thought he was an upright man with only two issues, sleeping with her and telling lies about his relationship with his wife.

Janay watched on for about five minutes before she decided to send him a picture text of the two of them. She thought about calling his cell, but she knew he wouldn't pick up so she decided on the picture text of them together. It was concrete evidence that he was busted. She made sure to zoom in and captured his lips all over A'saabi, showing the full facial features of each of them. She wanted him to see their faces because he knew how to swindle himself out of trouble. He was a fast, convincing talker. As she focused in on the two of them being so passionate a tear rolled down her cheek. She was hurt because she thought she was the one that held a special place in his heart. She felt betrayed by all his lies.

She had been with many men in her lifetime, but not one like Pastor. He was like the father she never had. When her father expressed himself it was always cold and harsh. Her father never held her in his lap, read her bedtime stores, kissed her on the cheek, told her how beautiful she looked, he never participated in her school activities, and not once could she ever remember him telling her he loved her. She was scorned because she had never experienced that daddy's little girl relationship. A relationship she felt all little girls should experience. A relationship that helped young girls understand what a young woman should look for in a significant other when dating and what to look for in a husband.

Pastor on the other hand was stern yet warm and compassionate to her wants and needs. He did demand that he was the head of their relationship. But, he always complimented her on how sexy she looked and dressed. Pastor knew exactly what to say to put a smile on her face and knew exactly how to turn a bad situation around. He always pampered her and made her feel like she was the one and only one in his life. Even though there was First Lady in the picture, he never compared her to his wife. When they were together it was always about Janay. He understood her better than anyone else and he knew her innermost secrets. Janay felt Pastor was her God sent soul/helpmate. She loved him in spite of all the wrong in the relationship.

She had just eaten lunch with Pastors wife, the woman that she wanted to hurt and belittle because of the way she flaunted her marriage. At that moment, her stomach churned at the scene before her. It hurt hearing First Lady speak about how affectionate and caring Pastor was, but that wasn't any concern to her because he was affectionate with someone other than the two of them. She was a cute, young, vibrant college student, his daughter best friend, and Deacon Jones daughter. She wondered what First Lady would do if she found out he was cheating with a young girl after she had given him so much praise at the luncheon.. Then Janay thought what in the world would Deacon Jones do if he found out his young daughter was involved with his best friend, Pastor Watson. The man he looked up to and would give his life for if it depended upon it.

Janay wiped her face, took out her cell phone again, focused in, and snapped the picture. She took about five or six to make sure she got all angles and ones that he couldn't deny. She made sure she got the one where he was kissing A'saabi while his hands were up under her dress. She hit send and waited to see if he would stop to check the message. As she looked over towards them Pastor moved his hand, leaned up reached in his pocket to retrieve his cell phone. The facial expression said it all and she knew that he knew he was busted. He looked around the parking lot he was in and as he turned Janay put the car in drive and peeled out her parking space. Pastor looked startled as he stepped away from A'saabi. That was one day Pastor would remember forever.

As Janay drove slowly towards her house she couldn't help but think how stupid she was to have given Pastor her heart, her time, her body, and her trust. She felt as if ten years was stolen from her life even though they'd slept with each other for only two years. She was devoted to him in all ways of a relationship. It was like a hard slap to her in the face that she had been faithful, honest, caring, trust worthy, and dedicated to married man. A man, who made a commitment to another woman, his wife, the First Lady of the church and a woman he loved. He had a family with kids, and a home that he was in no way intending to leave for her or any other woman without a fight. He manipulated her into believing he was unhappy, wanted a divorce, and not having sex with no one but her. It was all just a lie. Just an outright lie and he knew from day one that his story was just a lie. It hurt her so bad because she trusted him. Even more, because she believed that one day he would leave his wife and marry her. She was committed to their relationship that was built on lies and dishonesty. It was such a hard pill to swallow when she went into the relationship knowing that no good would come from such a deceitful deception.

Her black Mercedes sped down highway 75 north doing about 80mph with the music blasting, the sunroof open, and her mind on one thing only. Revenge. She wouldn't allow Pastor to steal her hope for happiness and a family. She knew she could get over the fact that he was wining and dining his wife since they lived under the same roof and pretended in front of the entire congregation like they had a fairytale marriage. She knew it would past, but to be involved with someone younger and prettier didn't sit well with her feelings. As the wind blew through her hair and

Monica CD played loud in the background, she thought of ways she would make Pastor pay for his dirty, low down, sneaky ways. She wanted him to feel the same horrible pain she felt and would be going through for a long time.

She turned onto her street and her cell rang. Looking down at the caller ID, she saw Boss pop up that was what she called him. He acquired that name because he was the boss in her eye. The name fit perfectly because he handled and ran everything as well as everyone. He was her boss at Greater Miracle Church of God so that part was true. She wanted so desperate to answer, but she wasn't ready to speak with him or see him because she knew he had a lie to tell as to why he was with that young girl. A lie that would be so convincing that she would forgive him and pretend nothing happened.

Janay ignored the three missed calls he made to her cell phone and he left such lengthy messages that each time they were cut off before he could finish. There were two text messages sent that resembled a chapter in a book that she deleted without reading. Janay knew he had a very ugly temper because she had overheard phone conversation with his daughters. She knew his text and calls weren't to say hello but to blast her for spying on him. She sent the picture with such an ugly message that read: 'you've fucked with the wrong bitch this time. Hell has plenty of room for devils like you. You will rot and burn in hell if it's the last thing I do before I die.' She didn't want to get into an argument with him before she could execute her plan to get revenge. She pulled into her garage, turned off her cell phone, and placed it back into her purse. She was done worrying about why Pastor couldn't practice what he preached. Why he wanted to play such nasty games with her life. But she was surely going to teach him a lesson about respect and trust. Something he hadn't practiced in their relationship or his marriage.

Never did it cross her mind that she was disrespectful and deceitful by being involved in an adulterous relationship with Pastor in the first place. She wasn't concerned with the fact she was disrespecting First Lady and his daughters. Being that he was a married man with kids and a public figure that many looked up to didn't sway her mind on her plans to ruin him. She had become somewhat close to First Lady and they occasionally spent time together, but for her it was to only keep up with what was going on in their marriage. All she was concerned about was getting revenge by any means necessary.

Janay was far from being the sweet innocent woman people viewed her as in the church community. Her past was like a well written play about adultery, betrayal, and deception. She wanted to grow up much faster than she needed and her father as well as her mother laid down rules she refused to obey. Once she graduated from high school in a small country town in Mississippi, she left home and moved to Dallas, Texas to become a registered nurse. Texas was the place to live an easily find a job in the nursing field. So, she packed her things and left to never look back.

Once she got to Texas it was like a new world being that this city was a lot faster than her little country town. She didn't know anyone when she first got there, but it didn't take her long because she was always a friendly person.

She was born Olivia Janay Smith, but once she moved to Texas she dropped her first name and went by Janay. She felt Olivia was an old, southern name that she felt would keep her from getting jobs and moving up the corporate ladder. She managed to get a scholarship so that took care of most of her schooling. She got a part time job working as a receptionist at a doctor's office her first year of school for extra income.

After her second year in college she realized that nursing would allow her to live well, but not the wealthy lifestyle she dreamed of. She wanted all the glitz and glamour that she read about and seen on television. Her first few months in Texas she had met many wealthy men that showered her with very expensive gifts for just a fun night on the town. She was like their trophy piece being that she was a very attractive young lady. So she opted to drop out of school and start an escort service. That business was very lucrative financially for her because she meet men of wealth that paid a pretty price to spend a few hours with women to fulfill their sexual fantasies. For a lot of the men it was just an opportunity to get away from the daily hustle of a long day at work before going home to a nagging wife with a house full of loud, whining kids. So, they opted to spend a few hundred dollars to get laid or just someone to listen to them and allow them to feel special for a change.

She had a luxury home, cars, clothing, jewelry, took many exotic trips, and had a very nice retirement nest. She hated the things she did to earn money, but she knew the nine to five, sun up 'til sun down job, couldn't afford that luxurious lifestyle. She hired several other women as the years went by and once she felt she earned enough money to start her own consulting firm and boutique. She sold out to one of the ladies that worked at the escort business and moved to Atlanta. That was a secret she intended to keep under lock and key. They say the best kept secret is the one you tell yourself.

A lot of people may not have approved of Janay's lifestyle and choices to make money, but she had a seven year plan. Her plan was to work hard at making enough money to give her a comfortable life. The first two years she set up and worked her plan to perfection. The remaining five years were to save and start her legitimate business. She was far from stupid when it came to business and doing the right thing. She knew the escort business was just a stepping stone to her paved plan. The plan was so well thought out that it only took her five years to accomplish her goals. While in the fifth year, Janay purchased a building, got a degree, and was well on her way to becoming a legitimate licensed entrepreneur.

Chapter Thirteen
Busted

It was over six weeks since A'Lexus and King officially moved in together and things were going great. She was excited that in a month she would be graduating high school and her plans were to attend Clark University the college close to her big sister. Through everything that had transpired at her father's home she still wanted to have them attend her graduation. She wasn't looking for an apology and surely had no intentions of issuing one. She wanted them to experience one of the proudest moments she would have in her life. The past was the past and that was how she wanted it to be. The Past.

King became the center of her attention. He was giving her total respect and treating her like a queen like every man should treat his woman. He ran her bath water, fixed her breakfast in bed, massaged her feet, gave her back rubs, held her in his arms until she fell asleep, and gazed in her eyes often. He was the true definition of a good man. Nothing close to what Roc was to Mercedes.

Roc was the scum underneath your shoe. He always lied, cheated, and treated Mercedes like crap. But, no matter what anybody said, Mercedes always defended him. He did wrong and she would dress it up to be something totally different just to make it look good. He was a true manipulator that knew exactly how cruel he was because he always said shit like, 'that bitch better not say shit to me about what I'm doing, she know better than to confront me, and I know she ain't leaving because she ain't got nowhere to go'. He knew he held the trump card in the relationship and he played it every time his ass was busted. But, like it's said you can only get away so many times before your ass get caught and brought before the judge.

The way her and King got together was so odd. Roc came home one night and didn't know she was in her room asleep because she had taken her car to the auto shop for repairs, and was dropped back off at the house. Mercedes had gone on another run for him so he thought he had the house all to himself. As she lay quietly in her room hoping he didn't come in there she heard the front door open, and then close. She knew he wasn't leaving because she heard him go in the master bedroom and start the shower. She eased up off the bed and tipped toed to the door that was slightly cracked. She could see down the hall that leads to the master bedroom. Her eyes widen because she couldn't believe what she saw. It was Porsha, her sister's friend standing in the hallway. Porsha must have taken her clothes off downstairs because she was butt naked. She almost yelled out at her, but she wanted to make sure she was seeing correctly. Porsha walked into the master bedroom leaving the door open. A'Lexus could see the silhouette shadow of her body walking towards the bathroom shower. Porsha opened the shower door and joined Roc. A'Lexus stomach churned, her breathing picked up, and she stood there in total disbelief. This is my sister's good friend butt naked in the shower with her man, she thought.

A'Lexus knew that wasn't the first time it happened because Porsha came in like she was invited and went right to what she wanted. Roc. She heard the moaning and sounds of two people making love. Tears were streaming down her face. She cried because not only had he violated her body he was really crossing the line by sleeping with his woman's friend in the house they shared, the shower they bath in, and in the bed where they sleep and make love. He was so disrespectful and foul.

She walked back over to her bed, grabbed her cell phone, and called King. She didn't tell him what his friend was doing because he always had an excuse or lie to protect him. Always saying his boy is not like that and he love her sister. She called and told him she wanted to see him and to just come on in because she was leaving the front door open. It took him less than twenty minutes to drive the forty five minute trip. He had been anticipating the day she would have a change of heart and give him a chance.

King opened the front door and was surprised that all the lights were off and his heart skipped a beat because he thought she had just called him over to talk and watch television. He wasn't expecting she really wanted to get down with him. He was excited because he really liked her, and wanted to make love to her from the first day he seen her but he wanted it to be special. As he topped the stairs the hall light came on and A'Lexus stood right in the doorway of the master bedroom. She had her cell phone ready to snap the picture of Roc and Porsha in the middle of making mad love. Once the flash snapped Roc pushed Porsha from off the top of him and Porsha turned looking shocked but never got off the bed or tried to run to hide.

She had an 'oh well' look plastered on her face. King looked like, what in the hell have I gotten myself into? As Roc pulled the covers over his lower part of his body and yelled out obscenities toward the door.

"Bitch what the fuck, are you doing?" He yelled as he stumbled to the floor.

A'Lexus didn't budge because she wanted him to hit her so she could call the cops and have him locked up. She had a witness and he wouldn't get away with it.

"Bitch, I asked you a question. What the fuck are you doing? This is my damn house and I'm tired of your trifling sneaky shit." He was pissed off and he wasn't backing down. Busted or not he wanted some answers.

"Roc. Man calm down." King tried to get him to cool off and step back, but it didn't work.

"You shut the fuck up because this bitch has crossed the line for the last mutha fuckin time! I'm tired of her shit. She gotta go and I mean not tomorrow, but tonight!"

A'Lexus tried to call her sister, but before she could dial the last number Roc had slapped the cell phone from her hand. "Keep your damn hands off me you bastard," she yelled back at him.

By this time Porsha was dressed and tried to ease pass all of the commotion. But, before she could squeeze past Roc and King in the doorway, A'Lexus walked up behind her and yanked her weave causing her to slip. As she fell,

A'Lexus commenced to beat that ass. She had her pinned down, pounding her in the face and chest area. King pulled her off, but she still swung and kicked. Porsha got up and ran down the stairs.

Yelling out as loud as she could at the top of her lungs, making sure Porshia heard her, "bitch! You better run. You're a trifling no good tramp. This shit ain't over. Trust me it ain't over. Wait until Mercedes find out your trifling ass was fucking her no good ass man." All she heard was the slamming of the front door, and then the car peeling out the driveway.

"So you think this fucking shit o.k.? Do you think my sister going to put up with your ass now that you've been busted?" She asked as she got up off the floor and walked toward Roc who was sitting on the edge of the bed.

"Fuck you bitch. Fuck you." He looked up at her with a look like he wanted to wrap his hands around her neck and strangle her.

"Man, chill out. Get some clothes on so we can talk." King looked like a deer in headlights. He couldn't believe A'Lexus called him to be in the middle of all this shit. But no matter what went on with Roc and his relationship with Mercedes he didn't want to be in the middle of any problems. He tried to stay neutral because Roc was his boy and since he became involved with Mercedes, they had become close. He cared for her like she was a sister.

"I'm good man, but this bitch needs to get her shit and leave my home. She can't stay another night under my roof. She's a trouble maker and I'm not going to put up with her ass anymore. I tried to be nice and give her a place to stay because she corrupted Pastor's house now she's trying to do that shit here and it ain't happening." He gave the most evil look as he walked pass A'Lexus who cried uncontrollable leaning on the hall wall.

"Man, it ain't that deep. She's just trying to protect her sister," King said, shaking his head and thought, why me lord? why me? King didn't want to be caught in the middle of this drama. He knew his boy would want him to lie for him, but he knew he was obligated to Mercedes as a friend also. But, he knew if he didn't make the right decision to tell the truth it would end his chances of getting with A'Lexus. He was torn between doing what was right and wrong.

A'Lexus ran up to Roc and spat in his face. He turned around and slapped her right across her left cheek. As she fell backwards, King caught her before she fell to the floor.

"Roc, what the fucks gotten into you man? You know the rule is to never hit a woman. Never man no matter how mad you've become. If you feel you want to hit a woman you just walk away from the situation. Never man and I mean never hit a woman." King was angry and upset with the action Roc took with A'Lexus. It had nothing to do with him being in love with her, but he was taught to never hit a woman. You walk away and give it time and if a man and woman is in a relationships can't work issues out through conversation they don't need to be together.

"You don't know this bitch like I do. She do shit, and then lie about it. I see she got the wool pulled over your eyes. I don't trust her and you better open your eyes because she is scandalous." Roc wouldn't even look at her. He started down the stairs, but before he made it half way down he hollered. "Help her get her shit because she has to go tonight."

"Don't worry, I'm leaving and best believe when I tell my sister about this escapade she will be leaving as well." She ran to her room and started slinging her clothes in the five suitcases she had in the walk in closet. King came in the room, stood in the doorway shaking his head as he starred in her direction. She was crying so hard she didn't realize he was standing there looking at her. She didn't have a clue as to where she would go. But she knew she couldn't stay under Roc's roof another night.

"Hey, calm down it's going to be ok." He walked over and pulled her next to him. He tried to hold and console her, but she pushed him away.

She pushed him in his chest to get him away from her and stepped farther in the closet. "Get away." You just like him. You saw him with her. You saw what I've been trying to tell you all along. He's a dog, a cheater, a dirty low down ass bastard. I hate him. I hate him."

"Can you just trust me?" He wanted her to trust him and give him a chance to prove that all men are not dogs. He extended his arms out for her to come to him.

"What am I suppose to do? Where am I supposed to go?" She looked confused, but knew she needed someone to hold her and tell her everything would be alright. She walked over and laid her head in his chest as he wrapped his arms around her. She cried like a baby.

"Don't worry about nothing. I've told you before, I got you.' I mean just that. Let's get your things and you can stay with me until you figure things out." He knew he was opening up a can of worms because his boy Roc wouldn't approve of him siding with A'Lexus, and then he would have to deal with Mercedes because she verbally told him to never mess with her sister.

As they left the house Roc looked, but didn't say a word. He had already thought of the lie he would tell Mercedes when she returned home. It wouldn't be any different from all the other lies except this lie had proof and a witness.

A'Lexus tried for two days to contact her sister, but the call kept going to voicemail. She prayed that the drug drop had gone as planned and she had made it back home safe and sound. This was unusual for Mercedes to not call and check in with her. She decided to just go over and let her sister know exactly what happened. She hoped Roc still left early in the day and didn't return until late at night. She got dressed and drove over to her sister's.

Once she got there she said a prayer before exiting the car. She walked up to the door and rung the doorbell and it rung about six times before Mercedes showed up to let her in the house. She felt a vibe coming from Mercedes that didn't set well with her.

"Hey sis, I've been trying to call you for the past two days."

"Call me for what?" Mercedes said with an attitude and acting really strange.

"I have something to show you and tell you. Can we go and sit in the great room?" She knew something was different with the way Mercedes acted and she couldn't put her finger on it. But, she knew her sister and knew something was wrong.

As they entered the great room Mercedes hadn't said a word. She walked in silence and didn't laugh or joke as she normally would when they were together."

A'Lexus tried to break the ice. "So what have you bought new lately that I can borrow?"

"Nothing. What is it that you want?" Mercedes was dry and to the point.

"Sis, I hate to be the one to bring this to you but when you were out on a run Roc got busted with Porsha having sex" she blurted it out so fast she thought Mercedes didn't hear all of it because she had the same look as she did when she opened the front door.

"Well, your story differs from Roc's. He said Porshia barged in the bedroom while he was showering and was trying to force herself on him. He said it must have been planned because you came in the room after he tossed her out the shower. He said he think the two of you were trying to have a threesome, orgy or just get your freak on but he wasn't a part of any of this charade," She was looking A'Lexus dead in the eyes as to be waiting for her to slip up.

"Sis, you have it all wrong. He's a liar and a cheat. He will tell you anything to save his ass. Why would I lie to you? I love you." She wanted to let Mercedes know that King was there, but she refrained from letting her know because she didn't know if King would man up and tell the truth.

"A'Lexus I've been there for you. I've been the mother you haven't had. Damn I've been the father we never had. I just can't grasp the idea that my own sister, my flesh and blood would stoop this low. I thought you loved me. Well I see you just like you're messed up father. You a sneaky liar just like him. I don't want to ever see or have anything else to do with you. Roc told me long time ago that you would try to ruin my life and relationship because you're jealous of me having a man to love me." She stood up and started walking towards the front door.

"Mercedes, do you really believe I would do this and do it to my sister? I love you and all I'm trying to do is protect you. All I'm trying to do is protect you." A'Lexus was in tears because she couldn't believe how brainwashed her sister was.

"Well, I got my man to protect me from people like you." Mercedes tone was rude and cold towards her sister. She didn't even look in her direction.

"What you mean people like me? I'm your sister and I love you. When have I ever done anything to hurt you, Mercedes? When Mercedes? When?" A'Lexus pleaded with her sister, but she just stood there with a look of disgust.

"It doesn't take but one time to cut to the core and you've done that to me. My own sister that I've taken in and taken care of and this is how you repay me?"

"So, all the times Roc has done some trifling shit that's ok with you. So every time he tell you a lie its ok? Every time he beats you its ok? I know he hits you and I've seen the bruises on your arms and back. I just hope it doesn't get to a point he goes overboard and something really serious happens."

"You know you're disgusting and Roc kept telling me over and over to put you out because you're nothing but trouble. But, I trusted you not because you're my sister and I loved you. You help family and they stab you in the back. You feed family and they steal from you. You let them live with you and your man and they sleep with him. Pastor was right when he said don't trust a sweet talker and a person that's begging because it's all a game and a lie."

"You would bring Pastor in to this conversation, and then talk about being a liar and a cheat. Well you should know because you've done them all. All I have to say is ask your lying boyfriend what he done to me. Ask him how he raped me and took my virginity. Ask him Mercedes how he took something I will never get back. How he stole the one thing I had a say so about. He will tell you another lie and you will believe him. I should be the one hurt because he took something I will never be able to get back. Never Mercedes." A'Lexus looked her right in the eyes because she wanted her to see the hurt and pain in them.

"Liar. Liar. You really hate what I have and any lie you can tell to destroy Roc you will say. You're disgusting and I hate you. I hate you, A'Lexus. I never thought it would come to this between us but this really does it for me. I want you out of my house and out of my life. I hate you." Mercedes starred at A'Lexus without blinking her eyes but the tears had consumed her thoughts. She was angry, hurt, and confused. Mercedes words were like a knife lodged in the carotid artery the main artery in your neck that supplies blood to your brain to keep you alive.

A'Lexus was shocked and hurt because she loved her sister more than anything. And, that trifling no good man tore them apart. She knew that whatever she tried to say her sister had her mind made up about doing what pleased her man. She stood up from the couch, looked around the room trying to find the words to say to her sister to try and make things better. But, she was lost for words as she looked toward her sister, but Mercedes had her back turned so she couldn't see her face.

Mercedes had said some cruel hurtful ugly things that sorry couldn't fix. Roc had done it again. He managed to twist the truth to keep him out of trouble.

A'Lexus opened the door to exit before saying, "I love you and will be here when you need me. I want you to know I would never ever do anything to hurt or harm you. Remember I'm your BSF for life." She walked down the steps, got into her car, and drove off feeling hurt.

Mercedes stood in the doorway, hoping it was all a dream and she hadn't heard the things her sister said about Roc. She hoped and prayed that it wasn't true, but she was torn between what her man had told her and how he had went into details how people want to destroy what you have because of jealousy. She reflected back at the pain she had just seen in her sister's eyes. The same pain A'Lexus showed whenever she spoke about the problems she had with Pastor. At that point Mercedes was stuck between a rock and a hard place. She didn't know whether to believe her sister or her man. She loved them both, but she knew somebody was lying, but which one? She didn't know.

Chapter Fourteen

Real Love

"Good morning, gorgeous," King said as he entered the bedroom wearing a pair of black and gray Sean John boxers, showing off his masculine physique that made her smile. He prepared her favorite breakfast that consisted of a steak omelet with extra cheddar and colby cheese, jalapenos, topped with tomatoes, picante sauce on the side, two buttered toast, and a glass of hand squeezed orange juice.

She raised her body up and leaned her back on the headrest of the bed as he laid the tray on her lap and took the napkin placing it on the top of her gown underneath her neck as if she was a baby putting on a bib.

"Baby, you're too good to me. I've never had a man to treat me this nice. And, I mean never," she said as she picked up a piece of toast.

He laughed. "What you talking about because I'm the first and only man you've had so that would make me the best thing you've ever had right?" He gazed at her as to be asking her a question and waiting for an answer.

"Yeah, yeah right. I meant to say you're spoiling me and I love it." She realized she had spoken without thinking and every time she did she always put her foot in her mouth and said things she should keep to herself.

"So what are your plans for today because I have to run some errands and hook up with my boy, Roc later to run some numbers?"

She rolled her eyes so hard King sat up and just starred at her. "Why you had to roll your eyes when I mentioned my boy, Roc?"

"I'm just tired of you hanging with him. I'm tired of the way he treats my sister. I just don't like him that's why I roll my eyes whenever his name is mentioned." She pushed the tray from her lap and got out of bed. As she started to walk towards the bathroom King jumped from the bed and blocked the entrance.

"What is going on baby? I know my boy got issues, but for you to be this pissed off about the way your sister is allowing him to treat her" Before he could finish A'Lexus snapped.

"What the fuck you mean how my sister allow him to treat her?"

"We both know she take up for him and she stays there when she can just leave if she's unhappy." King wasn't making it much better because it was more to her story and her ill feeling for Roc that he had no clue.

"Yes, she loves him, but that gives him no right to be an asshole and mistreat her. He's just a low down dirty dog." Tears streamed down her face and all she wanted was to get past King and lock herself in the bathroom to cry. But, he positioned himself in front of the door and refused to let her past him. That pissed her off more because she felt helpless and the man she loved so dearly just didn't understand.

"Baby, you have to admit that she's old enough to understand when things are right and wrong. Just like she got fed up with the way she was being treated by her father and she packed her things and left. This is no different. The only thing different was one was her father and the other was her lover. The treatment is the same." King looked her dead in the eyes as to make sure she understood the logic in what he had just said because she was torn between who was right and who was wrong.

"I guess with it being your boy you will take up for him and with Mercedes being my sister I have to be on her side. But, I know and you know your boy is wrong. It isn't fair that she have to endure the physical and verbal abuse. It's just not fair." She leaned into his chest and cried.

"I guess as you get older you will understand that in life we make the choices for our lives and we have to suffer the consequences from the wrong decisions. You can love your sister, but until she loves herself enough to get out she will have to endure the trials and tribulations. You can tell her over and over how bad it is, but until she feel she's had enough there's nothing for you to do, but wait for her to come to you for support." King tried so hard to say the right words to get A'Lexus to understand that her sister's worries were just that, her sister's.

"You don't understand King. You just don't understand that we're all that we have right now. Our parents don't care about us and we have to be there for each other."

"I do understand, but you have to realize that a lot of the problems that were at Pastor's house stemmed not from just his strict rules and behavior, but from the two of you as well. I love you, but I can't totally agree with you when you say that Pastor was the entire problem. You and your sister must first accept the fact that the two of you were a part of the havoc and hell in that house."

A'Lexus pulled away from King's chest because she couldn't believe the words she heard from her man's mouth. She stood in front of him shaking her head in disbelief. "How dare you accuse me and my sister of being the one's to cause the down fall of Pastor Watson's so called perfect home? You weren't there and you don't know what or why things got to this point. Just because you don't want to admit that your friend is an abuser don't try to throw it back on me and my sister. I see you're no different from him. They say birds of a feather flock together. So, I guess you're an abuser also." A'Lexus turned and ran from the bedroom. King didn't know whether to run after her or let her go and pout like a young, spoiled, teenage brat.

King knew he had touched on a subject that was still painful for her, but he had to shed light on the fact that her and Mercedes had caused a majority of the issues they had at home. He knew his boy had issues when it came to treating women right and he had spoken to him on many occasions to chill out. But, Roc was a man with his own way of doing things. Roc felt that any woman he dealt with had to understand and accept the fact it was his way or the highway. He grew up seeing his dad disrespect women and he never had the opportunity to experience a man and a woman in love the right way. So, in all his relationships he was controlling and abusive.

A'Lexus was lying on the sectional sofa in the great room when King entered the room. She wanted to get up and leave, but she knew he would follow her. As he sat down next to her he placed his hands over his head and leaned over towards her.

"Baby, I don't ever want to hurt you and I promise if there's anything I can do to help your sister I'm willing to do it. Just trust me when I say I love you". Tears came streaming down King's face. He showed emotions that made A'Lexus feel somewhat touched. He carried himself as this tough street guy, but deep down he had feelings and he was letting his emotions show.

Sitting up on the couch wiping her eyes with the edge of her top, A'Lexus looked away from King and started to cry. "King, I love you, too. But, I hate the fact that everyone think that it's me and Mercedes fault because of all the problems at Pastor's house. That's not true. Pastor has issues that need to be dealt with and he need to understand that we're his daughters who have feelings. First lady has never been the loving, caring, supportive mother that people thought. She's treated us as if we're the ones responsible for her and Pastor problems. Yes, we've probably done some things, but we're kids and kids do things. Baby, our parents have to understand that money is not going to keep a happy close knit family. You need to have love, understanding, be considerate of the each other's space, and be able to compromise. These things are not hard at all to accomplish."

"All I was trying to say was to never blame everyone else for your problems because in life when there's a problem between families, everybody has played a part in the problem. All I was saying was to analyze the situation and admit to the part you played in the problem. Don't use the fact that you're kids because the both of you are old enough to know right from wrong. At your age you do wrong because you still feel you can get away with it and if you don't then you have a problem with the consequences. If you do grown things expect grown consequences." Hugging her with a tight manly hug close to his chest, he tried to make sure she felt safe and secure. He wanted her to feel that if she ever needed anything he was there for her.

"I understand, but I still feel I can't just walk away from my sister when I know she needs me. I feel that I owe her that much being she has looked out for me time after time. I know without a doubt if I was in her position she wouldn't hesitate to come and rescue me from a bad situation." She still had that sisterly bond buried in her heart and nobody could make her feel any different about the way she felt this point. She had to be there and support her sister through the end and no matter how long it took Mercedes to come to her senses. A'Lexus was willing to be patient and wait until that time arrived.

"In no way am I saying to walk away and not be there for your sister. All I'm saying is allow her the space and time to realize the wrong in the relationship. Baby, if you keep pestering and pressuring her, she may turn on you for being in her business. It's hard for a woman to just let go and walk away from a relationship that she's invested so much in. She feels she just can't walk away and let another woman come in and take over all that she's built and accomplished without a fight. For her that fight's to accept the problems, work on getting them better, and moving on to the next phase of the relationship. But, trust me when she gets fed up with the bullshit she will walk away in a better state of mind and will be able to move on. This is called growth."

"What do you mean it's hard for a woman to just let go? If you know and see the wrong it's all about packing your things and leaving."

"Honey, its easy said than done, but women love with their heart, mind, body, and soul. Some men just love the physical attributes of a woman never allowing the love to flourish and grow. He's never attached to the relationship. So in a relationship when a man cheats, get caught, and just leave, he never really had an emotional bond with her. He cares for her, but he doesn't really care for her well-being. So, that's why it's hard for your sister to just leave. She's emotionally tied to the relationship and she has to allow her emotions to heal. Which can take some time or she can never get to the point of being fed up and end up staying in the abusive relationship. And, never letting go and moving on." King leaned back on the couch, hoping she understood. He knew this was too much for her to be absorbing at such a young age. But, he felt it was time she had some life lessons taught about love, relationships, emotions, hurt and trust.

A'Lexus was still caught up in defending her sister and wanting to be there to protect Mercedes and she kept talking. "Don't say what she can't do because she can. If it was the two of us I would be out and wouldn't look back."

"Yeah that is what you're saying now. Trust me if that time came in our relationship you would be trying to work it out or you would be trying to figure out a way to get me back while still here with me. You would be hurt, but you have to understand love is a strong and powerful four letter word. In a relationship it's very hard to turn off your feelings and just walk away. You may do it every now and then, but when I tell you once you open your heart and you encounter that sexual bond it's very hard. It's like the fluids from the sex is transferred like a blood transfusion to each partner and you start having a whole different outlook on loving that person."

Getting up from the couch, A'Lexus started walking towards the kitchen. "You can say what you want, but I know me. If you ever start doing the things Roc is doing, I will not hesitate on leaving. I don't know what other weak women you've dealt with, but I'm a totally different breed."

"Women as well as men can't all deal with deceit and lies. There is so much to love and letting go. People be in denial and really can't understand that their being abused. Their so into a person and the abuser knows how to lie and sweet talk them into believing it was a mistake and that they will never do it again. So they forgive them and make excuses as to why it was done or they flat out deny it's happening because of fear of the abuser or embarrassment of what family and friends might say. So baby as her sister just talk to her and let her know your there for her when she's ready to seek help."

"King, you really think you know what you're talking about, but I know my sister. I know that I need to get her out of that situation right now. I'm going to do this with our without your help."

"Baby, it looks like we're going to agree to disagree on everything when it comes to your sister and Roc. We're going to let them deal with their issues in their house and we're going to keep peace in ours." He said as he got up to follow her into the kitchen.

But she had to blurt out, "Roc is still a low down dirty dog no matter what you say."

All King did was shake his head and he knew then that she was the child at Pastor's house that always had to have the last word. He knew what Pastor and First Lady were dealing with in that house. Nothing but a sassy lip.

Chapter Fifteen

Always Daddy Lil' Girl

A'saabi knew that today wouldn't be a great day. It was the third Thursday of the month. The day Deacon Jones set aside for a father daughter day out. It was a tradition Deacon Jones set aside after her mother passed. Just the two of them bonding, and catching up without any distractions. Deacon Jones made sure to turn off his cell phone and not to schedule anything on that day because it belonged to her.

She felt that she was a bit too old for a father daughter day. By the end of the day it was all about Deacon being up in her business. Prying and poking in conversations that a parent should realize after a child moves out on their own it's not any of their business unless the child wants to indulge in a conversation. There was nothing wrong with going out to a nice dinner, maybe catching a movie, and then going back to their own home. But, it never ended that way. Deacon always ended up on A'saabi's couch, asking a million questions with most of her answers being well thought out lies.

As A'saabi finished up her makeup, her cell rang. She figured it was Deacon making sure she hadn't forgotten about their dinner date. So, she opted not to take the call. She walked into the master bedroom walk-in closet and starred at all the clothes, shoes, purses, and accessories in the closet. She felt blessed, but at the same time she felt like a spoiled rotten child. She remembered the comment one of her high school friends said when she stayed overnight and looked in her closet. She said it was a waste to have so many things that you couldn't possible wear and that it was a sin to be greedy when kids walked the halls of the school with tattered, torn and worn clothes. Those words resonated over and over in A'saabi brain ever time she opened her closet. She felt she could do something nice, have a yard sale and donate the money to a charity. She reached on the far left corner shelf and pulled down some studded jeans, studded tee shirt from Tags boutique, she walked over to her shoe collection and picked out some sandals she got from Garb Boutique in New Orleans when she and Mercedes went to the Essence festival. She loved boutiques because they carried items that you knew not everyone in the club would be wearing being that there were items that were unique and cute. She loved fashion and most of all she loved shopping.

As she got dressed, the cell rang again and that time, the doorbell chimed over and over, like a small kid was playing with it. She slipped on her jeans and threw her top over her head while pushing her arms through the sleeves with force. She rolled her eyes and stomped towards the door because she figured it was her father, showing up early as usual. Her daddy never was late. Not even one time in her whole entire life could she think of a time he was ever late. She wanted time to get in the mood to be bothered, but his pestering calls and showing up early ruined her me time. She looked at the phone that was still ringing, but decided to just greet him at the door with a fake smile.

She opened the door without asking who was there and her eyes bulged because this was surely an unexpected guest. She stood in the door with her eyes wide and mouth half opened because it was Pastor alone at her door. Before she could motion to let him in or say anything he grabbed her around the waist and gently pushed her back inside so he could enter and shut the door.   He kissed her so passionately, it startled her. She tried to pull away, but his strength over powered her. It wasn't that she didn't want him kissing her, but not in her apartment.

"Pastor what are you doing and why are you at my house?" She managed to muffle out the words as he continued kissing her lips and neck. But, he didn't say a word as he continued to force his kisses on her. He tugged and groped at her body like a mad man.

"Pastor, answer me now?   What are you doing? You need to stop right now." This time she was able to move her face to the left and get the words out clearer. "What are you doing?"

"Hush, and get undressed," he said as he tugged at her jeans' zipper and button, trying to get them undone. He tried to force her stiff body closer to the couch so he could possibly push her down and be in more control of her. A couple of times she swung her fist, hitting him on the side of the jaw and in the chest. But, that didn't stop him from trying to get her undressed.

"Stop it! Calm down and get your hands off me. I don't know what has gotten into you to be acting like this crazed man!" she said with a tone of fear. Pastor never been to her apartment alone and he never showed up out the blue, acting in that manner. She thought maybe he had an alcoholic drink and it had him acting strange. But, she knew she had to get him under control and out of her apartment before Deacon showed up because all hell would break loose.

"Why do I have to stop? Were you telling that bastard you been sleeping with to stop? Were you trying to stop him from having his way with your body? You must like what he is doing to your body," he blurted out as he pushed her away from him. His eyes were red and his breathing increased. He just stared at her and thought, nasty slut.

"What are you talking about? I have no earthly idea what you're trying to insinuate or accusing me of doing. You got the wrong woman and situation mixed up. It might be your other woman that's messing around on you." A'saabi was pissed that he had the audacity to come to her house unannounced and then accuse her of some bullshit. Something she had no clue about. The thing that bothered her the most was that he showed up unannounced causing drama like he really was her man. They had an affair with no strings attached. He had no right to barge into her home and make demands. Their relationship was a mutual understanding, that they would not become attached and fall in love. It was just a casual dating situation. They hooked up, he took care of her needs, and they went their separate ways.

"You know damn well what I'm talking about because the women in church have been whispering about you and this thug. I can't believe you would do this to me. I've bent over backwards for you and Deacon Jones. Don't you know if it wasn't for me you wouldn't have all these nice things that you don't have to work for or buy? I'm the one giving Deacon Jones that wealthy check every two weeks. I'm the one that made sure your college was paid for and the car you drive," he snapped at her.

"Pastor, what you do for my father doesn't constitute you coming up in here and forcing yourself on me. Nor does it make you have the right to preach to me about what you do and have done for my family." Tears streamed down her face and her body was shaking. She was pissed that he wanted to throw around the money he gave them. She never asked him for anything and she knew her father worked extremely hard for the check he earned. So it wasn't like her father was free loading on nobody. Her father, Deacon Jones bent over backwards for Pastor and Greater Miracle Church of God.

"I have every right because I will be damned if I allow you to mess around on me. I told you in the beginning that I'm not bringing anything home to my wife. When you felt you wanted to venture out and be with other men to let me know. I pay all the bills and gave you this lavish lifestyle and there isn't another man out there that can afford to take care of you this way. Not even your sorry ass father." A'saabi couldn't believe what she heard from Pastor. Mercedes and A'Lexus said over and over he was a ruthless, cold hearted, callus man. But, she never had seen him act that way. She always thought it was Mercedes and A'Lexus that caused all the havoc in their home. She finally saw the real Pastor Franklin Watson in action.

"Pastor you've said enough. You need to leave because we can never be anything other than passing acquaintances. You've shown your true colors. I can never love or respect you as a man and more so as my pastor. Please, leave now because my father will be arriving any minute and I do not want him to see you here," she pleaded with him even though she wanted to do something that would give her life without parole. If she could kill him and get away with it she would do it. But, she knew that it wasn't worth her risking her freedom over some dumb shit like killing Pastor. His day would come when he'd have to answer to all his wrong doing.

"You don't have to tell me his name, but were the two of you fucking. Do you love him?" Pastor eyes were red and his facial expression was tight. He paced the floor and his heart raced very fast underneath his shirt. For the life of her, she couldn't figure out what got into him and why was he all up in her personal life. He made it very clear in the beginning that his home and personal life was off limits.

"Listen, like I've told you before, you need to leave," she said calmly, but she was wishing he would just get back to acting like the pastor. The pastor all the church members had grown to love and adore. His actions were demonic and scary.

"I'm not going to play games with you and I damn well not going to be taking care of you and giving you money to give to that thug. He probably doesn't have a job or car. Probably getting money from you and using your car. That's how all you young dumb girls do. Let these bums use you up, and then they run off to the next dumb broad. You all will learn when it's too late."

Pastor was really saying some things that were making her angry. She thought about all the sweet things he said to win her heart. How he told her he would be there for her and would protect her. At that moment, he was the one that did the hurting. She couldn't believe he was treating her that way because she didn't do anything wrong.

She opened her heart up to an old ass man who she allowed to keep her from having a normal college, young girl's life. She committed herself to only him because of the rules he laid down in the beginning of the relationship. Stating he would treat her like a princess if she didn't get involved with anyone else, she had to get a routine checkup every month to prove she hadn't contracted any STD or incurable disease, she had to be home by midnight on the weekend, no male company at her apartment, or going out with guys even if there were other girls going. She allowed him to control her and she was becoming angry that she'd allowed him to steal her youth.

Her mind ran one hundred miles per hour. She thought about how they'd broken the Ten Commandments. How they were committing adultery, lying to his family, and congregation. She was hurting by all that she was faced to see but more so afraid of what Deacon Jones was going to do when it all surfaced.

"I just want you to leave my home before my father shows up." She was nervous because Deacon would show up any minute and she had no words to explain why Pastor was there. She was scared and her mind was blank.

"I should just wait on Deacon and see what he thinks about his lil' girl sleeping around with a thug." He was grinning out loud, sounding, like a demonic person.

Starring him right in the eyes she blurted out. "Why stop at the thug. Why not tell him about you and me sleeping together? I know that would be the best secret you could tell." She was pissed and angry that Pastor was allowing his jealousy to take him out of his pastor zone. Causing all that drama over what some women said in church. They probably were talking about his two hellish daughters because it wasn't a secret about the lifestyle they lived. But, he chose to come over to her house and disturb the peace. But, she wasn't going to allow him to ruin all that she had been working toward so that she could have a fabulous life. If he thought she would bow down, he better think again because he would see the real A'saabi that day. The quiet, shy, sneaky A'saabi would not let him ruin her chance to receive her college degree, or take away her lifestyle she loved. She was willing to fight Pastor tooth and nail if that was how he wanted it to go down.

"Pastor, I'm asking you again nicely to please leave my home. When you've calmed down, we can sit and discuss all this drama. My father is on his way over to my house and like I've said before he don't need to see you here." She spoke in a nice calm voice. Hoping he would understand and leave.

"Deacon is not coming over here. I called him and asked him to meet me in Savannah. I told him an emergency came up and I needed his assistance. You know all I have to do is say jump and he don't even ask how high. He just jumps until he thinks its high enough or I tell him to stop." He gave a smirk of a grin and leaned over to kiss A'saabi, but she turned away.

She feared what would happen next, but she tried to stay composed and talk him into leaving.

"Pastor, there's nobody else. You know how those women at church love to gossip and tell lies just to have a conversation stirred up. They see me as a young, single, college student that doesn't bring any young men to church so they make up lies to have a conversation about me. You should know better because of all the counseling sessions you've had to minister. Lies will cause disturbance in households. They will break up relationships, homes, and friendships. You should know all this and not get caught up in the he say she say drama. It was probably the same old messy members you have to sly way throw hints to every time we're in church." A'saabi tried her best to get Pastor to see where she was coming from so he could calm down and leave.

Looking up at him, she could see he was breathing regular, but she could still see anger in his eyes. He was a strict and stubborn man that always wanted things his way. He rarely gave into a debate and if he did he knew in his mind he was right and they were wrong. It was never a compromise or just ok you're right. Always his way and per him it could be no other way. Even if it was proven that he was wrong he would try to justify his wrong.

"A'saabi have you been with another man since we've been together? Is there someone else you're seeing or want to see? Have you had unprotected sex? How long have you known this man? Where did you meet him?" Pastor was rattling off every question that popped in his head. He wanted to know everything about this supposedly relationship.

"Like I told you before there's nobody. I haven't been involved with anyone but you. You should know this because with school, church, my father, and you, when do I have time for anything else? When Pastor?" She looked him dead in the eyes, waiting for him to respond.

"I know there's someone because just the other night when I rode past here there was a car in one of your parking spaces that stayed there until around three in the morning. When I came back through that morning about seven, it was gone. I know exactly who it was because I had one of the church members that work on the police force to run the tag." He walked over to the couch, sat down and waited patiently for her response.

She couldn't believe he was spying on her. But, her real concern was did he see A'Lexus come into her house because she was in King's 2013 black on black Camaro ZL1. Even if the car didn't have a tag on it anybody looking at it would picture a man behind the wheels. She was nervous because if he seen A'Lexus, that was another can of worms she would have to deal with later. But, he thought it was a man, what man was the question he wanted answered. She knew she couldn't rat her girl out, but she knew she couldn't take the rap for her either.

Thinking quick on her feet, she managed to come up with a good lie. "Just because someone parks in one of my parking spaces doesn't mean they're at my apartment. If you're talking about the new black Camaro with the chromed wheels, that's some guy visiting the girl a couple of doors down. Don't even fix your lips to accuse me of messing with that low life." She looked over to try to read Pastor's facial expression and to see if he was buying her lie. So far he seemed to look convinced, but the way he came in ranting and raving she really couldn't tell. He was a lot calmer, but she could see he still had doubt written all over his face.

Standing up and walking toward the door, he grabbed her tightly by the arm, turned her face towards him, looked her dead in the eyes, and said, "If I ever hear that you've been fucking around on me. I promise you that you and Deacon Jones will regret the day that you took your first dime from me. I put up with a lot of things but a sneaky person, cheater, and liar I will not tolerate. You had your opportunity to come clean if this was going on, but I'm going to take your word and pray that you're not lying to me." He opened the door and walked out.

She was startled for a few minutes because she had never experienced anything like that in her entire twenty years. Her father never displayed anger to her or any other woman for that matter. She was shocked beyond shocked to have the man she was secretively intimate with to be so disrespectful and rude to her. She always pictured the perfect relationship with someone that loved her, showered her with gifts, spoke kind words, and made her feel special at all times. This was all she knew when it came to a man loving a woman because that's how Deacon Jones treated her –with nothing but love and respect.

For a minute, it felt cute to know that Pastor was jealous. He always played that tough, stern disciplinarian role, but she seen something underneath all those layers of tough skin. He was a human hurting from a relationship gone bad just like everyone else going through a tough time in a relationship or marriage. He was hurt and scorned like a woman being cheated on.

Picking up her iPhone 5 as she entered the kitchen to grab a glass of water, she strolled through the missed calls to see if any were from Deacon Jones, letting her know he had an emergency to handle in Savannah. Strolling through the missed calls, there wasn't one from him, which worried her because that wasn't how he operated. He made sure to cancel and reschedule any of his commitments in a timely manner. He was true to his word and when he made a commitment he wouldn't let you down no matter how big or small it was. She checked her text messages and emails, but there wasn't anything from him.

She pulled up his number and hit the call button. The phone rung about five times and she thought it would go to voicemail, but her father's heavy, deep voice came in through the receiver. "Hello, Deacon Jones." He stayed true to his professionalism at all times. Even though the caller ID said 'Daughter A'saabi' he still answered 'hello

Deacon Jones' and ended each call with a quote from the Bible.

"Hi, dad, this is A'saabi, I was calling to see if you were o.k. since you never showed up for our date. Is everything o.k.?" She asked, trying to sound concerned.

"Yeah baby, daddy just had to run to Savannah to handle a few things for Pastor. I do apologize for missing our special time together, but Pastor told me he would be in the area and it would be best that the cancellation be done in person since our time together was so special and we've never missed one ever. So he volunteered to tell you in person so I wouldn't have to do it over the phone. He wanted to make sure if you didn't take the news well about the cancellation someone would be there to console you. But, I promise to make it up to you baby girl," He said, not having a clue about what all transpired.

Trying to play it off as tears ran down her face, she managed to speak "Daddy, you're the best father a girl could ask for and I love you so very much." She couldn't control the tears running down her face. Her emotions were so high. She realized that all the things her father tried to teach her about the mean, cruel world and about all the wrong men do was so very true. He told her that men that lied and cheated meant her no good. And men would say the right things, do the right stuff, and give you what they thought you wanted, so they can get what they were after, which is sex. He also said, they're not going into it for a commitment and to be faithful, all they want was to be sexual partners from time to time, and usually on they're schedule. He taught her to beware of those types of men.

But, somehow she managed to get involved with the man her father had preached about as being the wrong man. She felt used, but she knew she was the one to blame for that situation.

"Baby, I appreciate that so much, but I must say God has truly blessed me with one of the sweetest, kindest, most respectful daughters in the world. All twenty years have been a blessing because I haven't had to deal with the issues Pastor is going through with those two grown, mischievous, spoiled rotten brats. Baby, you don't let me down by disrespecting my rules even though you don't live under my roof still. A parent couldn't ask for a better child. Now, I must say I was scared once or twice when Pastor's daughters acted rebelliously. I really thought I would lose you in a war with them. Being that you were with them from time to time and spent lots of time in the church with them, I thought they rubbed off on you some kind of way. But, I pray and thank the Lord every day for covering you while keeping you on the right track. I commend you for being the strong, young lady that you are, to be able to cut them loose and continue with your life the right way. Baby, I love you and I promise to make this up." She could tell he was choking up because his voice had changed tones and she knew her father. He never showed his emotions to anybody. He could be having a really bad day but he always kept a smile. He could be hurting or had to deal with some major issues, he always stayed in deacon mode. He was always the happy helpful servant.

"Daddy, I appreciate you so much for everything. You have a safe trip back and call me when you get back. I love you dad." As she disconnected the call, she had a revelation as to what was a really good man. Her father.

A'saabi stood in the middle of the hall with the phone pressed to her chest as tears rolled down her face. She thought back to how she so innocently got involved with Pastor. She was at church many times after hours helping with fundraisers, programs, and youth projects. It all started her second semester in college and she didn't live under Deacon Jones' roof anymore. There were many times it was just her and Pastor finishing up last minute details and with her being young, quiet, and shy not any of the deacons, deaconess, ushers, choir members or First Lady questioned anything. Neither Mercedes nor A'Lexus knew anything about the affair. She had kept mum on all the scandalous things she did with Pastor.

She was there for all three sermons where he stood in front of his congregation and preached on infidelity, adultery, and fornication before marriage. Those were sermons that she sat through and knew what the Bible said a person should not do, but she allowed the devil to lead her down the path of lust, adultery, and destruction. She knew sinning wasn't right, but Pastor smooth lines had her convinced that what he said and did wasn't wrong. The Bible said if you ask for forgiveness it would be given.

She thought back to all the life lessons Deacon Jones taught her and the do's and don'ts in life. The main one was to never mess with a married man, even if he was living with someone and about to move out or just going through the motion. He always preached, don't let your reputation be the ruin of you succeeding in life and make you fall short of your blessings. He always told her that your reputation can make you or break you. That she would have to make the right decisions if she wanted to go far in life. Tears came down even faster because she knew that it could be the ruins of a great friendship with her two friends Mercedes and A'Lexus. The downfall of the church, the hurt and embarrassment First Lady would have to endure. All of the church members would struggle with their membership and the disgrace she would place on her father. The thought of hurting her father really made her angry and upset with herself. She never wanted to hurt him. He was all she had to love and depend on since her mother was killed. She felt she owed him for sticking in there and being both parents. He could have just walked away, but he did what was right.

Since there was no father daughter date and all the drama that took place, all she wanted to do was climb in bed to allow her brain to sort out some things. She needed to figure out how she would handle the situation with Pastor. She knew she needed to end the affair before something serious happened and everything fell like a domino effect. She wanted to call A'Lexus and let her know Pastor had seen King's car parked outside her apartment, but she knew if she mentioned it, A'Lexus would want to know why he was at her house. She turned on the television, propped the pillows up, and leaned back. She just needed some time alone to gather her thoughts on how she would put an end to their relationship she had with Pastor that had turned sour.

Chapter Sixteen

This Isn't Love

"Where are you going tonight?" Mercedes asked, knowing it was a question he wouldn't answer honestly. But, she thought she would ask because maybe he had realized that she was a part of his life since they lived together.

"Out," He said as he brushed up against her as he walked toward the walk-in closet. Never once giving her any eye contact or elaborating on his answer.

"Out where?" She knew exactly what she was doing. She was pushing his buttons and about to piss him off. She didn't care because in the last few months they hadn't been sexually active or spent any quality time together. The only thing they did was fuss and on a few occasions he had pushed her so hard she fell into the wall. There had been many incidents where he slapped her so hard with an open hand it bruised her cheek, back and nose, but the worst of the fighting was when he cold punched her so hard that her left eye bulged out, turned purple and black. For a day or two she thought she would go blind. On one occasion he hit her so hard it had caused a blood clot. Not once on any of the incidents did he apologize, but led her to believe that she was the reason he got so pissed and did those things to her. She loved him and overlooked his many faults because that is what Pastor preached. The man was the head and the woman is the tail and the wife should be submissive in her relationship. Maybe she had missed some of the sermons because there's nowhere in the Bible that say you should allow a man to beat you and disrespect you. But, from the looks of it, she was only living out what she saw under the roof of Pastor Watson. She loved her man and felt he was under a lot of business pressure while he took his frustrations home with him, but she was tired of the constant fighting, disrespect and lack of intimacy.

"Mercedes don't start. I told you OUT and that's all you need to know. What you need to be answering is did you run that package like I told you earlier?"

"No," she said nonchalantly as she headed toward the bathroom.

"What the hell you mean no?" He was irritated and pissed. He walked out of the walk-in closet and walked over to the bathroom door. "Answer the fucking question, bitch!"

Startled Mercedes jerked her body around to face him. "Who the hell are you calling a bitch?" Her nostrils spread, forming a fist with her hands as she walked away from the sink vanity in the bathroom.

"There are only two people in this house and I know I'm not calling myself a bitch," he spoke like it was ok with what he said as he backed out the door.

"I may be a lot of things, but a bitch isn't one of them. Don't you ever and I mean ever call me or anyone else one as long as you're breathing." She was all up in his face. That hurt like a dull knife dug into an open wound. He crossed the line for sure.

"You whatever I want to call you and I feel you're a bitch with some bitchy ways. All I asked you to do was drop a package off and your dumb ass couldn't do that simple task." Roc knew the things he was saying were hurtful and disrespectful, but he didn't care. His main concern was that the package wasn't delivered. He hadn't lived in a Huxtable home. His dad was never in a committed loving relationship so he knew nothing about respecting a woman, being faithful, or being a decent companion. All he knew was the mean cruel streets.

Mercedes was so pissed that the man she allowed to strip her away from her family, her studies in college, her friends and most of all her respect for herself didn't respect her enough not to call her out of her name. He said it like it was ok and she should be ok with it also. But, she wasn't.

"Roc, I'm sick and tired of you using me to run your drugs. I'm tired of you not being here with me or for me. I'm tired of you beating me and talking to me any kind a way. I'm tired Roc. I'm sick and tired of all this bullshit you've been taking me through." Tears rolled down her face like a bucket of water had been turned over on her head.

"If you're so sick and damn tired why not get your shit and leave?   Oops I forgot your sorry ass don't have anywhere to go." Smirking as he took his index finger and pushed her nose, moving her face to the side.

She was fuming. "I can go stay with my sister." But, she thought of how ugly and disrespectful she had been to A'Lexus it brought tears to her eyes.

"Once I tell my boy how trifling you are he will not let you come up in his place and your sorry sister will be kicked out as well. He's already tired of her whining ass anyway.   Like I've told you over and over Pastor not having either of you back in his house. So, you better get your act together or get the fuck out." He pushed her so hard she fell over the chair that she uses to read her books. Before she could get up, he reached down and yanked her by the arm pulling her up, but with his force she landed on the edge of the bed. The top half of her body was hanging from the edge of the bed and the other half dangling on the floor. She managed to slide to the floor which allowed her to get her balance and stand back up.

"You're ruthless, and evil, but trust me, payback will get the best of you and you will..." Before she completed her sentence he slapped her again. That time, the sting from the slap numbed her left side of her face and she let out a loud scream that caused her eardrums to ring.

"You need to learn to shut your damn mouth when you're ahead. But, you always run your damn mouth like you know every fucking thing and don't know shit. Just shut the fuck up sometime." He said as he leaned down to be in her face. His hot breath smelled of weed and alcohol.

"Stop putting your damn hands on me. I'm not your fucking punching bag." She still managed to speak after he almost distorted her jaw bone. She had her right hand holding it, trying to sooth the pain as she looked at him and rolled her eyes.

"You need to get your ass dressed and make that run. I don't want to hear your sorrow ass excuses. Just do what you've been told to do and do it now. I'm so fucking tired of you and this trifling attitude you have every time I'm around you. That's why I hate being here." The words he spoke were like a knife piercing through her chest.

"I told you before I'm done with that bullshit. I'm not going to jail for you or anybody else." She had managed to get up off the floor and move over to where the mirror was so she could see her face. Tears refused to fall from her eyes. It was either from the sting she received from the slap, or her nerves that triggered tears was numb, or her body was just immune to the beatings. Either way she knew she was tired of the abuse from him. She didn't know why he always felt he had to deal with an issue with violence, but she wouldn't continue to be his punching bag. He would either stop on his own or she would have to handle him the best she knew how and that wouldn't be nice.

"Listen, you not done until I tell you that you're done. Right now I need you to stop all the bullshit talking and get your ass on that run. With all the shit you've caused don't expect to be paid." he said as he reached over to pick up his cell phone to make a call.

She walked over to the walk-in closet, grabbed the luggage, and placed it on the floor next to the bed. Walking back toward the dresser, Roc grabbed her wrist and held it so tight she could feel pressure in her chest. "What in the hell do you think you're doing?" He said as he squeezed even tighter.

"I'm leaving what part of me getting the suitcase and putting my things in it you don't understand?" She said as she yanked away from him and started stuffing her things in the suitcase, pretending he hadn't said a word.

"No, you don't understand. I said get your ass on that run. Not when you feel like it. Right now, not later," he said as he pushed her wrist to her chest and used all his force to push her into the wall.

"Roc, you're hurting me and you need to stop before I get hurt." Then he punched her in the stomach, causing her to ball over, putting both hands out as if she was trying to grab him to catch her balance. But, really she was trying to fight back. His abuse was something that has been going on from the time she moved in to his house. It seemed as if his space had become compromised and he didn't know how to just openly say he didn't want her there with him. It started with the verbal abuse that led to the emotional abuse and now it was a full blown physical abuse.

She still loved Roc and would give him the world if she could. She felt he was just dealing with all the stuff in the streets, the people that worked for him not having the money on the date he requested or always coming up short, and all the drama that came with being the top man in the drug game. She felt he was under a lot of pressure and it caused him to react with fighting. She knew she couldn't go to the police and tell them about the early morning late night fights. She couldn't be seen with the black eyes, purple and black bruises so she stayed inside the house until they healed. She would lie to her sister and best friend about why they couldn't come and visit.

About two weeks after a beating incident, A'saabi pulled into the driveway just as Mercedes was walking down the driveway to the mailbox. She was about ninety-five percent healed. Since the swelling and deep, dark color almost fading away, she was able to say she bumped it opening up the kitchen cabinet. A'saabi looked at her rather strange, but never questioned her further about any details. Mercedes knew if A'Lexus had been the one to see the faded bruises the truth would come out. That was one thing about A'Lexus; she never allowed stuff to slip past her. She would have asked a hundred questions, played the undercover detective, and snooped around the house. She would go into protect mode and call all times of the day trying to make sure Mercedes was o.k. and show up unexpectedly until she got concrete evidence that nothing happened. That's one thing about, siblings; it's very hard to not protect each other.

"Ok, I will go this last time and make this run, but we will talk when I get back about you making other arrangements with your package pickups and drop offs. I'm tired of doing this illegal shit and you should be, too.

You're getting too old to be hustling, ducking, and dodging. This is played out and you need to think about changing your life and settling down." She pulled on her jogging pants, grabbed her tee shirt, and yanked it over her head with a lot of force. As she reached to get her sneakers she felt him yanking her ponytail causing her head to tilt backwards.

"Don't tell me what you not going to do. I make the decisions around here and don't you ever and I mean ever not do what you're told when it comes to you handling my business. My shit is on the line and folk not getting paid because of your trifling ass. So get your shit together and get it done." He took his index finger and poked her forehead with all his force as he turned to walk out the room.

Sobbing as she tied her sneakers, she wanted so bad to just pack her things and leave. But, she knew if she did leave that would leave Pastor as the winner in this battle of who was right. She felt she couldn't endure anymore of the abuse, but knew she had to find a way out of this horrible nightmare she lived. But, what could she do when she had no money saved, no place to go, and the car Roc purchased for her would surely be taken back once she left. She had to come up with a plan to get some money and move out of his house first. The thought made her heart feel heavy and mind pause for a few minutes because she was blank with ideas.

She normally would take A'saabi or Porshia on her road trip, but she needed to be alone so she could think about all the torture and hell she dealt with. Why she allowed it to happen for so long? She knew that wasn't the type of relationship she wanted, especially with all the street sense she had, she knew she should have kicked him to the curb long time ago. But, she tried her best to make it work and she tried so very hard to be understanding. But, she was the victim once again at the hands of a man.

As she walked down the half winding staircase she could see Roc in the dining room removing the art from the wall so he could go into his hidden wall safe. He kept his very important papers, a few of his hand guns, and stacks of money in the wall safe. She was never given the safe pass code, so she really didn't know how much money or the details of the documents. It did cross her mind several times to try and get inside, but she didn't know if he had it rigged and an alarm would go off. So she never tampered with it.

She spoke in a soft, low voice under her breath as she opened the front door to leave. "I'm leaving and will be..." Before she could finish her sentence he walked toward her. He forced a few hundred dollars in her hand and turned to go back to what he was doing at the safe.

"What the hell this suppose to be for?" she mumbled as she looked down to try and count the money on the sly. She wanted him to think she really didn't want it, but at the same time she didn't want to cause any more drama. She just wanted to get in the car and drive off far away from him, the house, and the problems.

"It's fifteen hundred dollars to gas up get a hotel when you get there, and a little extra to buy you something," speaking as if he hadn't done a thing and everything between them was like when they first met. He was strange like that. Beat your ass one minute, and then act like this loving, caring man. He needed counseling, medication or better to be institutionalized

"Yeah, ok." She knew right then that only about two hundred was going to be used on gas and a room. The rest was going into her emergency fund. She realized that she had to get it the best way she could and by any means necessary. Making runs would make her some fast quick money, but she had become tired of fearing getting caught and risking going to jail. She knew if she got busted Roc wasn't coming anywhere near the jail to get her out. Pastor Watson and First Lady most definitely wouldn't come to get her out. The only people she could possibly count on were A'Lexus, her best friends A'saabi her ride or die chick.

She got into her Mercedes, pushed the button to let the sunroof back and turned up the radio as she backed out the garage. She knew this be a long trip that she really needed to think some things out. She had an idea, but she needed to make sure she dotted all her I's and crossed all her T's before she made any major moves.

Reaching into her Michael Kors bag, she grabbed her cell and placed it on the charger. But, as soon as she reached for the adapter her cell began to ring. She looked at the caller ID and saw it was Porsha; she quickly hit the delete button. She called back two more times before she left a message. Mercedes erased without even listening to them because all she wanted to do was give some sob lie about being sorry for screwing her man. She wasn't in the mood to be forgiving her trifling ass; she had too many other issues that were more pressing of her time.

As she drove, she thought about all the ugly things she had said to her sister the last time they seen each other and she felt bad. She hesitated for about five minutes and decided to give her sister a call. She had the car phone dial A'Lexus cell number as she drove. The phone rung about three times before A'Lexus picked up and Mercedes just blurted out in the middle of A' Lexus saying hello. "Hi sis, what's up with you today? I've been meaning to return your calls, but I've been so caught up with errands and things to do around the house." A'Lexus was stunned to hear Mercedes voice on the other end. She had called her several times, but Mercedes didn't pick up or respond to her voicemails. Not, one call to meet and talk about the situation.

"I've been busy and I'm out running some errands right now. I've missed you so very much, sis," A'Lexus said, trying to sound cheerful and excited to hear from her sister. But, deep down she was still angry with Mercedes for how she talked to her and allowing them to get caught up in the thug fast life. But she wasn't looking for an apology, just a conversation to figure out how they had gotten to such a bad place.

A'Lexus knew that no matter what bad situations she was facing she was still going to the prom, still going to enjoy her classmates on senior day, and continue preparing for graduation. Even though, she was still in high school, shacking up with a drug dealer that wasn't going to change her plans. She also knew this wasn't the life Pastor or First Lady wanted for her, and surely not the lifestyle she had envisioned as a child growing up but this was the life she had dealt for herself so she had to make the best of it.

"A'Lexus, I'm so very sorry for the things I said and did the last time we seen each other. I hope you will accept my apology. I'm sorry I took you through this drama filled unhealthy lifestyle. I really see just what you were saying about Roc and that I deserved to have better. I really apologize for hurting you and not seeing what you tried to tell and show me about the unhealthy abusive relationship. I admit I was blinded by love and I promise to you to get out." Mercedes was having a revelation because she had destroyed her life and in the process she had torn their family to pieces. She didn't have a relationship with her father, mother, and then she was feuding with her sister. That wasn't right and she knew it wasn't, and she knew she had to start somewhere with making amends. So why not start with her sister whom she loved unconditionally.

"Mercedes, I forgive you and I hope you know I do love you. All I ever wanted for you was the best. I never meant to overstep in your relationship but when you hurt, I hurt. I'm here for you for whatever and whenever. So don't you ever feel you can't come to me because I love you and would do anything for you?" Her words were softly spoken because she had been waiting on that moment when her sister had gotten fed up with Roc's trifling ways.

Mercedes was speechless because she never thought in a million years that her sister would forgive her for all the problems she has caused in her life. She really screwed up and she needed to make amends with A'Lexus, First Lady, and most definitely her father Pastor Watson. Having to ask Pastor Watson for forgiveness wouldn't be an easy task because he was stubborn and not an easy person to bend. He was set in his ways and when he laid down the rules' they were written in stone. But, she knew in order to get back in the good graces of the Lord she had to do what was right and she knew that it would be a process to redemption.

"So where are you headed Mercedes?"

Mercedes cringed because she really didn't want to lie to her sister again but she knew she couldn't tell her she was still making a drug run for Roc. So she vowed to herself that this would be the last lie she told her sister. "I'm headed to pick Roc up to run a few errands."

"You know I will pass on this outing if he's going. I really wanted to hang out with you and catch up because we haven't been together in a minute. But, I can wait to be with my BSF. I love you."

"A'Lexus, I love you too. I promise I will make all of this right. I promise you this on everything I love." Mercedes was sobbing so hard because she knew that if she would have just followed Pastor few rules, not any of these bad things would have happened to her and her sister. She really felt horrible, but she knew she couldn't go back and erase any of the past. She had to make it right.

"Well I guess I'll let you go run your errands and talk with you later. But, you have to promise me we will hook up later this week. Love you and be careful," she said, sounding sad. She really wanted to see her sister and catch up. But, she knew she and Roc were like oil and water, so she did what was best and kept her distance. She hit the end button on the phone and thought how strange the conversation was with her sister. She knew something was different about their call, but she couldn't figure it out.

Mercedes turned up the volume of her car stereo to hear the sounds of Kendrick Lamar blaring through the speakers. She shook her head because what he belted out described just what she needed to ask the Lord to do for her sinful life. When it got to the part about 'sometimes I just don't understand,' she felt the tears streaming down her face. She knew she had sinned and come short of his blessings, but she knew from the words Pastor preached that all you had to do was ask for forgiveness and it shall be given. She had done so much sin that she didn't know where to begin asking and she didn't know which sin was the worse.

She was actually applying Pastors sermons to her past, present, and what her future would be like if she would just change her situation. It wasn't going to be easy and she knew that she first had to admit to herself the wrong she had done before she could get the help and forgiveness. The tears were streaming down so fast she couldn't keep up trying to wipe them from her face. She couldn't believe she wanted to go to her father and tell him she was sorry for all the wrong she'd done to him and the family. All she wanted was for her father to wrap his arms around her and letting her know everything would be alright. Like he would do when she was young and had problems. She wanted him to hold her close to him while telling her that he loved her and to say a prayer asking the Lord to wash away her problems.

Her thought was to call Pastor and ask if she could come and speak with him. But, her second mind told her to focus on getting out her bad situation, and get the package delivered to get Roc off her back.

As she drove she really had the urge to call Pastor because he had always been the one to heal the pain, kiss the boo boos, and make her feel better by protecting her from harm.

She hit the button on the steering wheel and used voice dial. As the lady completed her speech she said Daddy, she heard the automated service keying in the numbers, and then she heard the ringing. She got nervous because she really didn't know what to say to him. She hadn't seen him since the day she left the house and they hadn't had a phone conversation in months. She took it upon herself to call First Lady, but most of their conversations were lectures on First Lady getting the courage to stand up for her rights and to find her purpose. Mercedes purpose was to shed light on the already messed up family situation and to hopefully get her mother to see that she was more than just a the lady in church sitting on the front pew. And that, she was Tiffany Watson, a strong woman of worth, full of potential with a purpose to do and be whatever she wanted to be in life.

"Pastor Watson," his base tone voice said through the receiver.

There was silence from her because she couldn't bring herself to speak.

"Mercedes, why are you calling my phone? Your calls are not welcomed."

She wanted to hang up, but she didn't fear him anymore. "Hi, daddy. I was just calling to see how you and mom were doing?"

"I don't have any money to give to you or your sister. By now the two of you should have jobs to take care of your financial needs. I made it clear that if you wanted to be grown then you do just that and be grown."

"Daddy, please tell me why you always have to be so cruel and evil? I was just calling to tell you I love you."

There was a silence on the receiving end of the call. Pastor was lost for words, but he managed to say the wrong thing as usual. "I'm busy. Call me some other time when I can talk." He did just as First lady. He disconnected the call.

Mercedes pulled over on the side of the road leaned her head on the steering wheel and just cried like a baby. She cried because she realized the mess she caused her once so perfect life. Out of all the schemes and lies she couldn't find the right way to fix it. But, she wouldn't allow Pastor to just hang up without her telling him just how she felt and what she had been through.

She redialed the number and it rung about five times before he picked up. "Mercedes I told you I was busy."

"Well, father whatever you're doing will have to wait. I feel I'm more important and you should realize that family comes first. I really need my daddy right now." She hesitated before she could bring herself to finish. "I'm sorry, daddy. I'm so very sorry for ruining our family, my life, and A'Lexus life. Can you please forgive me?" She pressed the volume for the phone on the steering wheel so she could hear his words clearly.

"Mercedes, sorry don't make things better. You have to be willing to change you and your life in order for forgiveness to be given. People use sorry too loosely and they usually use it when their in trouble or they feel guilty about something they've done. I'm hurt by the way you disrespected me and my home. I'm hurt that you almost ruined our livelihood. Something I was doing for US. Us Mercedes." She could hear in his voice that he was really hurt, but cared.

"Daddy, I'm sorry so please forgive me. You always said you live and you will learn. Well, I'm going to admit that I was wrong. All I'm asking for is for you to forgive me."

There was a pause before he spoke. "I've already forgiven you and I've prayed every day for you and your sister. I left it in the Lord's hand the day you both left."

She could hear in her father's voice the pain he felt. All she wanted was to get back in good grace with him. She knew she needed to change her life before things got worse.

"Father, I know this might be a bit much to ask, but I wanted to know if A'Lexus and I can come by the house so we all can talk."

"That sounds good. I will have your mother to contact you with a day and time." Mercedes wanted to ask why he just couldn't say come by anytime, but she knew she was pushing it. So, she settled with having her mother call her to make the arrangements.

"O.k. That sounds great." She paused. "Daddy I love you."

There was silence, which seemed like an eternity. "I love you, too." And the phone went dead.

She rolled down the window and drove off to her destination. She felt that even through the bad there was always some good to come out of it all. The pressure of what she dealt with at home with Roc seemed senseless and she knew she had to get right with herself before she could change her bad situation. But, she knew it wouldn't go down without a fight when she told Roc she was done. She knew that even though he didn't really want to be with her, he wasn't going to just let her walk away without some drama. She knew she had to be prepared for whatever the outcome would be with them. But, she did know she wanted out.

Chapter Seventeen

Reflections

The breeze from the early morning air was a breath of fresh air for First Lady. She rarely sat out on the patio early in the morning, but she had so much on her mind. She had to finalize the plans for the Women's Retreat, which she and the ladies were hosting. She had scheduled an appointment for the interior decorators to come and change out the color scheme and furniture in the master bedroom and bath. A change that was long overdue. The last change had been about three years. She felt the warm chocolate and teal blue was so outdated. She wanted something much lively and colorful like some hues of yellow, gold, sage greens, or lavender, and pink. She thought change might get Pastor back to his old, freaky ways. Ways he hadn't displayed in the bedroom in quite some time.

First Lady sat in the recliner and reminisced about how before they got married their sex life was like two cats in heat. How he couldn't keep his hands off of her and made sure to please every inch of her body completely. She yearned to have her body wrapped in his arms while he caressed and kissed her most intimate spots. Never in a million years would she have thought he would lose interest in her. She kept herself looking attractive at all times and she was submissive to his every beckon call. She loved Pastor and knew there wasn't another man on earth that God would want her to be with even if he crooked over and died.

As she looked over the balcony she saw the water in the pool ripple with waves. That gave her a calm state of mind even though she couldn't help thinking about how Pastor changed. He wasn't' the same vibrant, romantic man she met over twenty-five years ago. His demeanor was different, his conversations were totally different, his circle of people changed, and the loving, caring man was no longer apart of him. There was something different and she couldn't put her finger on it just yet. She knew if he kept doing the things he was doing, eventually something would come undone and the truth would come to light. She knew not to pry or go snooping for answers because Pastor always said if you go looking for something, you bound to find it. You might see something that you don't want to see. So she stuck with the old saying 'what you do in the dark will surely come to light and it was just a matter of time.'

When she was pregnant with Mercedes her gut told her Pastor was cheating and with all her hormones running rapid, it was in her to find out the truth. So, she spied on him to only find out something that would destroy her trust for a very long time. He kept the same late nights, avoiding any sexual contact, blaming it on the fact she was pregnant and he didn't want to hurt the baby. Always having to go outside to hear when his cell phone rang or needing to go help one of his friends that were having car trouble in the

Lies & Deceit

middle of the night. First Lady was fed up with the lies so she trailed him one night. He ended up at a hotel across town and when she caught a glimpse of the lady he met, she felt horrible. The woman was gorgeous and with her being fat and pregnant she thought that was the reason he didn't want to be affectionate with her.

For weeks this bothered her, but she couldn't bring herself to let him know she spotted him with the other woman. Being involved in the fast life, he met all types of women so this was something First Lady understood came with the relationship. Plus, there would be late nights, lots of going out to the club, getting up in the wee hours of the morning to make a run, house being bolted down with locks and chains for their protection as well as all types of guns, plenty of money to be hid, the best alarm system money could buy, and from time to time he would fall into the arms of another woman. That was understood when she got into the relationship. But she prayed he would never be intimate with another woman, she trusted him to be faithful.

It finally came out about the other woman and in a way she never suspected. A suspicious letter addressed to her with no name or return address was in the mailbox. She was hesitant at first because of all the anthrax in the news she didn't want to take a chance. Once she opened the letter she thought it was a prank because it was written on some paper ripped from a notebook with the raggedy edges written in a red pen. As she read the letter her blood pressure elevated and thought she was going into early labor. The letter was from the other woman and she went into detail on how she met Pastor and how they had an affair for almost two years. The letter went on to say that she was sorry for causing problems in their marriage, but it was only fair she told her the truth about everything. She wrote that she was pregnant and Pastor was refusing to accept the child. He told her it would be a cold day in hell before he took care of her baby and that she needed to get an abortion. She went on to tell how he said he loved his wife and the only baby he would care for was the one his wife was carrying. She explained how she had messed up her life, her parents had refused to be there for her and how she had allowed pleasure with a married man ruin her life. She said she was keeping the baby and didn't want him to have anything to do with the baby, but wanted to send First Lady the letter letting her know her child would have a brother or sister somewhere and maybe as they got older the adults could come to terms and let them get to know one another.

At first, First Lady wanted to go and choke the other woman, but she knew that wasn't going to solve the issue. She was married and pregnant by the man she loved, but he had cheated and had made a love child. She was angry and wanted revenge, but she knew that being totally upset with the woman wasn't fair because it took two people to have the affair and make a child.

She decided to meet the woman one afternoon to find out all the details. She was hurt that Pastor had told her he was unhappy at home. He only married her because she was pregnant and he was doing the right thing by marrying her. It was lie after lie he had told to this lady. She explained to First Lady that if she would have known he was married she would have never gotten involved with him.

Her and Jessica exchanged cell phone numbers and vowed to stay in touch for the sake of the unborn kids. Being that they were both so close on deliver dates they didn't want the kids growing up dating if one was a boy and the other a girl.

To this day Pastor had no idea she had talked with Jessica or did he know that she knew A'saabi was his biological daughter. That was part of the reason she made sure growing up Mercedes and A'Lexus spent time with her to build a relationship. Many people would make remarks that they looked like triplets, but she graciously smiled and said thanks whenever they were out in public. She figured Pastor knew A'saabi was his biological daughter because of the bond he had with Deacon Jones. But neither man knew she knew about this little secret. She vowed to never let the cat out of the bag. Once Jessica was murdered she made sure she did everything possible to see that A'saabi had the things she needed and some of the things she wanted. That's the reason she gave Deacon Jones the extra money every month.

Pastor had lost all contact with Jessica after she told her parents she was pregnant and they told her she couldn't live in their home any longer. She packed her things and contacted him to see if he would help her, but once he refused to give her any help she lived from friend to friend houses until she met Deacon Jones. When she was dealing with Pastor she didn't go by Jessica, but her middle name Elaine. So Pastor never knew Deacon Jones wife Jessica was his baby mother and A'saabi was his biological daughter. He did see the resemblance in the girls, but it never crossed his mind A'saabi could actually be his daughter. The story Deacon Jones told about his wife dying two years after his daughter was born made him think she was Deacon Jones daughter.

Deacon Jones never knew who A'saabi real father was because Jessica never told him any details only that he was a big time drug dealer and he didn't want to take on the responsibility of being a parent.

Chapter Eighteen

Blame It on Me

Mercedes knew she had to get a confession from Roc about all the incidents of unfaithfulness and especially the incident with her sister A'Lexus. He had been out all day but she had made plans to stay up and wait on him to get home.

It was about midnight when she heard the car pull in the driveway and the garage door go up. She sat up on the couch and turned down the volume on the television.

Entering drunk and high as usual, he walked in and went right to the kitchen. Mercedes got up off the couch and started towards the kitchen behind him.

As she entered the door leading to the kitchen he turned and blurted out. "Why, the fuck you always following me?"

"That's your problem you always thinking somebody following you. If you weren't doing foul stuff you wouldn't have that worry." She snapped back at him.

"You keep that smart shit up and your ass will come up missing. I'm not in the mood for all your bullshit. It's too late to be hearing your shit."

"I just want you to come clean about all the bullshit you've been doing and have done." She looked him dead in the eyes and didn't crack a smile.

"Like I told you before you don't question me about nothing I do. I'm fucking grown and you don't take care of me. So let's get that understood right fucking now. I take care of you." He said as he grabbed a beer from the refrigerator and brushed past her as he walked toward the family room.

"Did you sleep with my friend Porsha?"

"Don't question me."

"Answer the mother fucking question now." She yelled at him.

"Ok, yeah I fucked your friend. Now, what else you want to know." Snickering as he said it.

She held back the tears because she didn't want him to see her pain. "Did you rape my sister?" She hesitated because she really didn't want to hear the answer for real.

"Bitch, I raped your sassy ass sister, I fucked your friend Porsha and I fucked A'saabi. Now you have the truth now leave me the fuck alone."

Mercedes heart stopped beating. He had to be lying about A'saabi too. But it registered that he said he had raped her sister. The word rape made her blood boil. He had violated her baby sister and taken her virginity without her consent. He was foul and deserved to be punished for his trifling whorish ways.

"You're a low down dirty dog. You deserve to rot in hell because you've crossed the lines of disrespect." She tried hard to keep the tears from falling. She refused to let him see her breakdown from all the horrible things he was saying.

Roc jumped off the couch and lounged at her but before he could reach her she pulled out the gun she had in the waist of her pants. She pointed it at him. "If you dare try to put your hands on me I will kill you."

"So you will kill me. The man you love and that's taking care of you when your own trifling father won't give you the time of day. You want to kill me." He laughed as he spoke.

"I will let this lead burn a hole in your ass if you don't get the fuck out of this house." She aimed it right at his head. She wanted to shoot him in the brain because she felt all the trifling acts stemmed from his thinking. She wanted to see him suffer the same way he had done to her and her baby sister.

"Bitch, you know you not going to pull that trigger. You full of talk, you don't have the guts because you a weak bitch." He said as he stumbled towards her.

The word 'bitch' kept ringing in her head and she had told him before to never call her that word. She looked at him and said "I'm giving you one opportunity to apologize and promise to never use that foul word to me or anybody else." She starred at him waiting for him to respond.

"You out your fucking mind if you think I will ever apologize to you because you are a Bitch. All you ever were good for was a good fucking and nothing else."

"You're a sorry excuse for a man. I see exactly what my father tried to teach me about no good assholes like you."

"How the fuck your father going to tell you some shit like that about no good men. His ass is the main one that's no good. He fucked my mother, he killed my father and he screwed your best friend. I bet your ass didn't know all that shit. Now what the fuck you have to say."

"Liar, Liar, you don't have anything better to say, so you try to use that lame as lie. Fuck you."

"You can believe what you want but I know the truth. He was my father's best friend. They sold drugs and ran the streets together. I was in the car the night he killed my father. He killed him and ran, but when he looked in the car he thought I was asleep. Ask him about it. I can tell him the story better than he can tell it. We've had our drug run-ins from time to time. You mother was an escort for years until she started her own escort business. She was a whore. And when I fucked your best friend she kept calling me Pastor and when I confronted her she confessed. So who's trifling? I guess it's not me anymore." He stumbled and fell over on the couch.

"I don't believe a damn word you're saying. You always try to twist and turn things around to get it off you. It's all a lie. You can't ever own up to your wrong doing. You have to tell lies to try and get out of everything. My parents never did the things you're saying, and my best friend isn't sleeping with my father. You're just trying to use the people I love so much to try and hurt me. Well it's not working." Tears rolled down her face, she was trembling and the gun swayed from side to side. She didn't want to believe any of the things he was saying.

"Hold up I'll prove it to you." He reached in his pocket and dialed a number.

"Hello." A soft voice came through the receiver. Mercedes looked stunned because it was A'saabi voice.

"Hey, this Roc, I was calling to see if you and Pastor Watson were still fooling around. I have a nice attorney friend looking for a really nice lady and I thought about you."

"So funny you should ask, because there was a situation between the two of us and I'm ending the relationship with him this week." She spoke softly in the phone.

"Well, give me a day or two and I will hook you up with my friend." He said sounding so convincing.

"Thanks. Hey, thanks for not letting my best friend know about us. I know if she found out she would probably kill me."

"No problem." He said and disconnected the call. He looked in Mercedes direction and he could see the rage in her eyes.

"How could you do this to me? I've bent over backwards for you and you do this to me. Out of all the people in the world to sleep with, you chose my best friend, my friend and my baby sister. How could you be so cold and callus, you deserve to die." She pointed the gun towards his head but she knew she couldn't kill anybody. She hated him but not enough to give up her freedom. She knew in due time he would get his.

"I want you to get your shit and get out. I'm not going to allow you to just continue to disrespect me."

"This my fucking house. You get your shit and leave." He said as he got off the couch and tried to grab the gun away from her.

When he knew anything Mercedes had taken the butt of the gun and smacked him across the side of his head. He grabbed his head and realized he was bleeding. This angered him. "You fucking hit me." He blurted out, still holding his head and trying to rush up to her.

Lies & Deceit

This time she kicked him between the legs. He took the other hand and grabbed the inside of his legs and fell to the floor. She stood over him and gave him an ultimatum. "Get your shit and leave or be carried out in a body bag. These are the only two choices you will get and if you take too long I will decide for you."

He scrambled and scooted towards the door. He pulled himself up, opened the front door and stumbled out.

Mercedes body trembled and shook so hard. She was so torn by all the things she had heard. She didn't know what to believe at this point. She knew for sure that he had slept with her two friends, he had raped her sister and that was the worst truth she heard because her sister would have to live this story over and over.

She heard his car leave out the driveway and she felt some type of relief that the storm was almost over.

She went into the master bedroom gathered some pajamas and went to take a shower. As the hot water from the shower splattered on her body, she scrubbed as if she could wash away the layers of disgrace and pain. After about thirty minutes of showering she exited, dried her body and put on her night clothes.

Mercedes rolled over in the queen size bed in the quest room and just laid there starring at the wall. She had been sleeping in the quest room ever since the incident between her and Roc. Lately, she had so many thoughts going through her mind. As she laid there her body felt numb and lifeless.

Chapter Nineteen

And I'm Telling You

Tiffany couldn't believe the words she was hearing from the partially closed door to Pastor Watson's office. She wasn't in no way sneaking and trying to eaves drop. She was headed to his office to take him his dinner since he claimed to be so enthralled in writing Sundays' sermon. As she approached the door the conversation struck her by surprise because he was calling someone honey, baby, and saying things he supposed to be saying to her.

She stood outside the door unnoticed for about fifteen minutes. She wanted to walk away and give him his privacy, but when he said to the other person on the line he didn't love her anymore and that it was just a matter of time before the divorce was final. It struck a nerve because that was the first she had heard of getting a divorce. They never had a conversation about separating or getting a divorce. So that was a shocker to her and she felt she needed to get some clarification on his conversation.

Before she decided to barge in she wanted to see if from the conversation she could tell who he was talking to on the phone. Her mind started to scan the church isles, the phone call log, the woman that pranced more than twice on Sunday, trying to get the his attention and the woman that always volunteered for extracurricular church activities. She came up blank because she made sure that any activities at church she was the head person.

"Janay, I love you more than anything. Haven't I told you this over and over? Look at all the lavish things I've given you. Baby, I love you and would never cheat on you. That picture you sent me of that young girl kissing on me in the parking lot wasn't what it seemed. She threw herself on me. I promise baby that it's only been you that I've given my love. You don't have anything to worry about because I'm going to make you the official First Lady Janay Watson very soon." He was really pleading his case to her.

Before First Lady knew anything her hands became weak and the tray slammed to the floor spilling all the food as it made a loud crashing sound. It startled her, but not as much as it did Pastor because he jumped and cursed.

She was busted, but it didn't matter anymore because she had heard everything she needed to hear. He was a liar, a cheat, and a disgrace. She was so hurt because she felt betrayed by Janay. The woman she had opened up to and allowed to become a woman in her circle. She manipulated her and smiled in her face while she was screwing her husband. She felt violated and betrayed by them. They say you can't bring women around your man, and every eager woman that wants to be your friend only wants to know your activities to map out her game plan. Those that hate you most likely have their game on lock. The rule is to trust no one.

Pastor came storming out of his office with a frown, but as he entered the hall First Lady had turned and ran back to the main house. She ran because she was hurt and devastated by the things she heard him say. He said a lot in that short period of time. It would take her a while to dissect and really understand just exactly what he meant.

The bedroom door slammed as Pastor Watson rushed into the room with anger and frustration displayed on his face. That sent chills down her spine and at that moment she had a flashback of her days living in the world of being an escort to many men. That was a past she hated to relive because of the abuse and awful things she had to endure just for that dollar. A dollar she earned by any means necessary to live a ritzy lifestyle.

Pastor Watson was angry and commenced to hit her without telling her why. The back handed slaps to her body made her curl up closer to the wall she had resorted to because of the lashes her husband inflicted upon her body. She cried and whimpered under her breath because she knew no matter how much she cried, yelled, and begged he wasn't going to stop until he was tired. She had encountered beatings far worse in the escort business she owned years before marrying him and she learned over the years that there wasn't much she could do or say. It was a business you knew exactly what you were getting into so you accepted the situations and circumstances.

In the escort business you learned the word ENDURE very quickly. So, she dealt with it the best way she knew how and that was to let him get it out of his system. Once he was done he would usually leave the home for a couple of hours, giving her enough time to wash her body of any blood, doctor on any bruises and cry her pain away. He always returned as this caring loving husband not admitting to any wrong doing. Pretending as if nothing ever happened that needed to be addressed. She knew she needed to leave the abusive marriage, but she had two daughters, she loved the lavish lifestyle, she was a First Lady at the church and plus she didn't have a paying job. She had learned to accept the problem and move on.

He spoke harshly as he planted two slaps to her back. "Why the hell I have to keep telling you the same shit over and over about being sneaky and eavesdropping. Why?"

She didn't know whether to respond or keep quiet because either way she knew she would be slapped again. If she answered he would slap her for opening her mouth saying she was being disrespectful and if she didn't respond he would slap her even harder because he would say she was ignoring him. She was in a no win situation, so most of the time she kept quiet and that way she wouldn't be accused of saying the wrong thing.

"I know you heard me ask you a question woman? Are you deaf and dumb? I'm so tired of this shit with you." He pushed her head into the wall, leaned down close to her face, and spit on her cheek.

A tear rolled out of her left eye onto her cheek because there were many abusive things she could endure, but to spit in her face wasn't one of them. She pulled her hand from the side of her hip, balled her fist up as tight as she possibly could, and pulled her arm up so fast it shocked her when she wailed her fist across the side of his arm. The force stung her knuckles, but she was more upset she missed his face. This was what she was aiming for, but once he spat in her face he leaned up, so she only caught his arm and part of his side.

She knew this would be a roller coaster of a fight because she had never hit him back or made an attempt to fight back. One thing about Pastor Watson he made it very clear he gave orders and he was the only person to do any lashing out. She had become bold and before he realized what happened, she took her foot with her six inch heel and rammed it into the inside of his thigh.

He grabbed her ankle and yanked her down in a lying position, but she was kicking both legs so hard he couldn't hold on to the grip he had on her ankle. As he stepped away from her wailing legs he screamed. "Woman, what in the hell has gotten into you?" His eyes were fiery red. He was breathing hard like he had just finished a morning jog.

"I'm sick and tired of your lying, cheating, and abuse," she blurted out sounding like a woman fed up. Her heart was racing, but she didn't back down.

"You don't fucking talking to me in that tone and if you would ever raise your hand up at me again. I will…" his sentence was cut off by her angry voice.

"Or you would do what? This is the last time you ever put your hands on me. I'm fed up with all this fake lifestyle, all the lies, all the trifling things you do and say to me and my daughters. You've beat my ass for the last time and I mean the last time." She stood up and she walked over to him. She had woman'd up on him.

She stood up to him and it felt damn good because she felt she had allowed him to control her for far too long. Maybe it was the harsh words Mercedes preached to her about taking a stand for her life and demanding to be treated with respect. She use to feel powerless, but at that moment she felt empowered to do what was right for her and her daughters. Something she had neglected doing for a very long time now.

"I don't know what the hell has gotten into you, but you better release it right now. You know you've stepped completely out of the realm of your wifely duties as a pastor's wife. I'm not going to tolerate it."

"Pastor, no Franklin, I be damn if I allow another minute to past having you disrespect me in the manner I just heard. You can have your trifling bitch and all the others that you claim was throwing themselves on you. Because I don't want or need you any longer."

Before she knew it Pastor had backslapped her across the cheek. It caught her off guard and the hard sting made her reflex and she punched him so hard in the right eye. As fast as she punched the right eye her fists were pounding at his head. She didn't know what had gotten into her, but she felt good releasing all that built up anger.

He threw his hands out to try and stop her from punching him in the face. All she saw was him falling to the floor grabbing his private area. She didn't realize during the fighting she had taken her right foot and kicked him between his legs. He was in a fetal position, letting out loud screams, begging her to stop.

She leaned down in his face and in a low tone, and said, "If you ever and I mean ever think you can hit me. You need to think twice because I'm not the wifey you use to have that you controlled like a puppet. If you ever mistreat my daughters again I promise you that you will regret the day you said I do. I know you're not treating your bitches in the street this way and I be damned if you think you can come in here, disrespect and fight me. " She got up, walked out the master bedroom door not even looking back to make sure he would be ok. She headed to his office that was off limits to her and the girls, but today she was going inside to see what and why it was off limits. She would deal with Janay at a later date, but for now she needed to know what was so secretive in Pastor's office.

As she took the long walk down the hall towards the office First Lady started reflecting back to the beginning of how she met Pastor, getting married, having kids, starting the church, the many sacrifices and changing who she really was in order to be First Lady. The tears rolled down her face as she started to realize that her daughters were subjected to live a life they had no choice or say so because this is what Pastor wanted for them. A life he had mapped out to get rich with the family having to come along as part of the plan and suffer the consequences. She cried as she reflected back because she knew what Mercedes had told her all along was the truth, but she didn't know if she could mend the broken relationship with her daughters and this bothered her the most because they needed her then and more so during that time.

She entered the office and looking around she remembered ordering the curtains, the carpet, picking out the paint color, arranging the desk, and chair. Hanging the wall pictures and placing his name plaque on the desk as well. Those were the fond memories she had of the office that was off limits to her, but being the obedient wife she never disobeyed and entered his space. Looking around everything seemed to be in the same place, but he had added a few of his own touches like paper weights, a mini golf course in the corner, and another set of chairs for his church members that visited or had an appointment.

Something caught her attention very quickly. It was a picture of A'saabi and Pastor together. She starred at the picture because it wasn't taken at the church, at their house or at Deacon's house. First Lady had a chill come over her because she thought he knew all along that A'saabi was his biological daughter and just kept the secret to himself. She hadn't told him and she knew Deacon Jones didn't have a clue. Just maybe Pastor realized his responsibility and had stepped up as a real man. She was unraveling lie after lie as she looked around the office. She found several hotel receipts, boxes of condoms, love letters that didn't have a name on them. She was hurt and she felt the saying if you go looking, you surely will find what you don't want to know or see. She felt she needed to stop looking because things were getting to be a bit much for her. She was hurt, but relieved at the same time. It felt as if layers of hurt were shed from her body.

She continued to ramble through Pastors desk and the more she looked she became more upset and hurt by the lies that were being unraveled, but most of all the trust she had given him and the marriage. She had allowed him to steal her real happiness and to betray her right in front of her face. The most important thing about the relationship was that she loved him, but she was tired of the abuse. Nobody knew of the many fights, arguing and the pain she felt behind closed doors of their home. She lived a life full of lies and deception. They would be secrets she would take to her grave.

The lifestyle she lived was too glamorous and enticing to just walk away from without a fight. All her life she had dreamt of having since she was about fifteen years old. She had finally achieved the dream life, and she wasn't about to let a few angry episodes, a cheating spouse, a trifling adulterous home wrecking woman take her away from it after she had put in all the blood and sweat. It was a situation of leave what you have and go to something you don't know. She had sacrificed and worked hard to obtain this lifestyle and would be damned to allow another woman to just waltz up in it and try to ruin it. She was ready for Pastor, and he'd better come prepared for war, because she wasn't going out without a fight.

She turned the lights out in the office and before she closed the door she looked around it one more time to make sure she wasn't leaving any undisclosed skeletons.

Chapter Twenty

What You Do In the Dark

The weeks prior to Mercedes making amends with her father had been nothing but drama. Roc had threatened Pastor in front of her. He told Pastor he knew he was the one that had murdered his father and that he was a bullet away from hell, if he continued to butt into his business or relationship with his daughter. Pastor, didn't take kindly to his threats but allowed him to vent his anger. Pastor felt he needed to get it off his chest because he was living life in a pair of boxers soaked in gasoline.

First Lady had confronted Janay about the affair with her husband. She told her that it was only a prayer she prayed that saved her from giving her a royal ass whipping. And if she ever heard mention that they were alone or even speaking with each other they both would pay the ultimate price, and it didn't come with change.

Janay confronted Pastor and gave him an ultimatum. That in one week she wanted him to handle his unruly wife or else he would suffer some consequences. She also told him that if she ever heard anything about him and A'saabi, or any woman, she would be doing some serious time in the penitentiary. As usual Pastor brushed it off as a woman scorned and thought it was flattering.

King had a big blow out with Roc because of the way he treated Mercedes and disrespected his woman, A 'Lexus. Once A' Lexus told him that Roc had raped her that was the last draw for him and their relationship. King vowed to kill him if he ever looked twice at A'Lexus. Because there was no forgiveness in his book for abusing a woman, he had witnessed his mother getting abused growing up.

A'saabi confronted Pastor and told him that if he ever mentioned anything about their relationship, he would regret it. She told him that if he even tried to mess with her father's salary or job he would pay dearly.

The city of Atlanta was hot with drama and anything could go down between the feuding friends. But each of them tried their best to keep their distance from one another.

****

Mercedes sat on the chaise lounge in the family room at her parent's house smiling, because she had finally realized that her life was worthy of nothing but the best. She was happy that all she had done wrong was being made right. Her relationships with her sister, mother and father had been restored and they were on the road to making the Watson's family resemble that of the sitcom The Huxtables. She was happier and realized she was really blessed to have such a wonderful family.

One thing she couldn't quite put the pieces to the puzzle was that of her mother's sudden change. First Lady had started to voice her opinion with Pastor when she felt he wasn't right. She had taken on more activities and started doing the things she enjoyed without his approval. First Lady and the girls were spending more quality time together. They were going out on lunch dates, shopping sprees and had taken several mother daughter trips to other cities. All this pleased Mercedes because this is how she felt a mother and daughter relationship should be in life.

Her relationship with her sister was stronger than before and they vowed to never allow anything or anyone to come between their sister-hood, especially a man. A'Lexus was so excited that all her family could share in her special day and attend her graduation. Mercedes had planned a surprise family and friend cookout the weekend before the graduation. She wanted to do something special for her sister because she realized the importance of family. And to never take family for granted, no matter how devastated or drastic things became between family members.

Now on the other hand, her relationship with A'saabi still needed some working out because she had trusted her to be a friend and not a backstabber. She loved A'saabi but she felt that their relationship had been tested and she needed time to sort some things out. A'saabi felt horrible about the things she had done and knew just saying 'sorry' wouldn't fix or make it better. She had contacted Mercedes on several occasions and tried to mend their friendship. But Mercedes just wasn't ready to open that door back up for her to come into. Mercedes knew she eventually would make amends but when was the question. She didn't hate A'saabi and she didn't want to be apart from her because she had been a true and loyal friend until she crossed that trust issue by sleeping with her man. That was truly the ultimate NO NO in a friendship.

Her relationship with King was still good. She respected their relationship because he was true to his friendship to her. He loved his boy Roc but he didn't pick sides and was fair with anyone he came across. Even though she didn't like the idea of him having a relationship with her baby sister, she appreciated the fact that he treated her with respect and loved her unconditionally. Even after all she had endured in the relationship with Roc, King still stayed true to his relationship with her sister. King told her that friends come a dime a dozen but a true friend will never cost you anything in life but happiness and loyalty.

Porsha and Roc was totally kicked out of her circle. She refused to allow these two people to have any more space in her life. She was completely done with the drama they brought into her life. She loved Roc but loved herself enough to walk away from his abuse and disrespect, because she knew if she would have stayed any longer, somebody was going to get hurt far beyond just a slap, kick or punch. She was glad that she was spared any pain for herself or her family before it was too late. She knew that Porsha would never change her ways because she had been abused at an early age, by her mother's boyfriends, her uncles, and her male friends cheating on her. Porsha was scorned and out for revenge. And until she found help for her problem she would always be running game on somebody. So Mercedes knew that if she kept these two people in her life, she would never find peace and success. Her only thought about them was that just maybe they were meant to be together, because two wrongs will never make a right.

Roc had threatened many times that payback was a mutha fucka and somebody would pay for the hell he had endured all his life. He told her that he didn't care who got caught in the rapture of his fury and that it was going to be plenty of pain endured by someone. Most of the time when he spoke those threatening words he was either drunk and high, so she always brushed it off.

The only issue she had about mending the broken relationship was that of her father. He had claimed to forgive but said forgetting would take some time. They spoke but there was always that 'but' in the conversation, that always kept them with a wedge in the relationship. He had changed but he was still strict with his rules. His rules still applied but it was something different with the way he handled things around the house. He spoke to First Lady in a different tone, he didn't keep his late night excursions, and he did more family activities. He was different for sure but Mercedes just couldn't put the 'why' to the question. She was just excited to have the family back together.

As she got up off the chaise lounge to answer the door, there was a breaking news report flashing on the television hanging over the fireplace mantle. Being that the volume was on mute, she couldn't hear what the news anchor was reporting. The doorbell rung about two more times, before she was able to reach the door to answer. Opening the door she looked startled because there were two officers standing in the doorway.

"Yes, may I help you?" She said in a low soft tone. Looking at the officers and wondering why they would be at her doorstep.

"Yes, is Mrs. Watson home?" One of the officers said as has he was raising his head from reading his notepad.

"No, she's out on some errands. Is there anything I can assist you with today?" Mercedes responded back, getting nervous because the cops weren't smiling.

"Do you know when she will be returning home?" He said looking very stern and standing in a poised position.

"She should be home shortly. Is there a problem officer?" Mercedes was looking rather nervous because this wasn't just a routine call. There had to be something serious going on for them to be standing at her front door.

"Ma'am, we really need to speak with your mother. Is there any way you can contact her and find out if she's headed home?" The other officer that had been standing silently looking down the entire time said as he lifted his head to make eye contact.

"Yes, but can you tell me what is the nature of the visit?" Mercedes said getting nervous because neither officer flinched.

"Make the phone call and see how close she is to the house and once she gets here we can explain our visit." The officer said as he starred at Mercedes not blinking.

Mercedes asked the officers to stay put while she went back into the house to grab her cell phone and make the call. As she was entering the family room the breaking news was ending and she caught a glimpse of a body lying in a pool of blood. For a minute she thought it resembled King but the body build was too large.

As she walked back to the front of the home she heard her mother's vehicle pulling into the driveway. As she opened the front door she could see the officers walking over to approach First Lady. Mercedes picked up her pace and tried to reach her mother the same time as the officers, so she wouldn't miss the reason they were at her home.

First Lady looked shocked as the officers reached for her mother's car door. Looking confused she slowly opened the car door and one of the officers assisted in helping her out the car.

"Mrs. Watson, may we speak with you inside your home?" The officer that had been doing all the talking said, as he waited on a response.

"May, I ask as to why you're at my home sir?" First Lady said looking totally shocked and confused.

"Ma'am we really need to speak inside. We would like for you to be sitting and comfortable." The officer said trying to get her to understand that the issue was very serious.

"Yes, let's go inside." First Lady said as she led the way back to the house.

"Sir, can you please tell us what is going on. What you have to say, you can tell us right here." Mercedes blurted out, because she felt they were prolonging the reason they were at their house. She wanted to know why they were there, and why they were taking their time to tell them the reason.

"Mercedes, just hold up. They will tell us." First Lady said in a shaky voice. This was the first time Mercedes had seen fear and nervousness in her mothers' voice and eyes. She had experienced her mother being stressed and upset about how Pastor treated her, but not this type of uneasiness.

As they entered the great room, First Lady sat in the first available chair. The officer that had kept quiet most of the time began to speak. "Mrs. Watson, I know you're wondering why we're at your home."

"Can you just please tell us why you're here?' Mercedes blurted out loudly. She was getting frustrated by the fact that they had been at her home all this time and they still didn't know anything.

"Mrs. Watson, there's been a murder in the downtown city of Atlanta and" The cop said as he walked closer to First Lady. First Lady screamed out loud and Mercedes sat there in total shock that startled the police and he stopped speaking.

Mercedes brain was twirling fast trying to figure out who could be dead. Her thoughts focused on the bad people in her life. Was it Roc, Porsha or King? She wondered who it could be if it wasn't any of those three people. In the midst of going blank she missed the conversation the officer had with her mother. As she looked over to her mother she saw her mother just starring in total shock.

The officers exited the house and all Mercedes heard was the car pulling out the driveway.

The only thing First Lady kept saying was "Oh, my goodness. No Lord, please please tell me it's not so." After about a minute of screaming and hollering First Lady passed out, never answering who had been killed, why or how.

www.ingramcontent.com/pod-product-compliance
Lightning Source LLC
Chambersburg PA
CBHW051458170626
46811CB00002B/532